Ding
and
His Extended Family

Stewart Davis

PAGE PUBLISHING
Conneaut Lake, PA

First originally published by Page Publishing 2024

ISBN 979-8-89157-977-4 (pbk)
ISBN 979-8-89157-990-3 (digital)

Printed in the United States of America

CHAPTER 1

Arrival

"We're here! We're here!" the excited little Cinnamon barked.

"Will you shut up!" Sassy yelled as she woke up. "You have said that every time we stop!"

Ding yawned. "What's? What is all the barking about?" asked Ding.

"That stupid little—"

Ding was quick to interrupt Sassy. "Don't say it, Sassy!"

"I'm really sure this time! That this is our new home!" Cinnamon still barked with excitement.

Just as he finished talking, the door on the moving truck opened. "Come on, you three! We are finally here. This is going to be our new home," said the sergeant as he moved the seat so the three of them could get out.

Cinnamon, the little Chihuahua, was the first to quickly jump down off the seat and leap out the door. As Sassy jumped down out of the vehicle and looked up, she barked, "*Wow!* Ding, hurry up, you have to see this!"

"I see it. It has to be the biggest backyard I have ever seen!" Ding barked as he stared out the door of the moving truck. He had never seen a yard like this before. He was used to his little yard, where he could see the other homes just over his fence and hear the other dogs barking in the neighborhood. This was nothing like that, for as far as he could see, there were no other homes around, just a house and some buildings. He was so overwhelmed that he just sat there in the truck, taking in all the new sights and smells.

"Honey! What's wrong with the dogs?" the wife, Wendy, asked.

"I think they are in shock! They are probably thinking this has got to be the biggest yard they have ever seen!" he answered. "Come on, you three, there's a lot more to see and explore. You're no longer going to be city dogs. You're now going to be farm dogs."

"I think they are going to like it here, Mom!" said the youngest daughter, Anna. "And look, there is a pond with some ducks."

"Ducks! Oh no! Mommy, we have to make sure that Sassy doesn't see them," cried the older daughter, Chey.

"It's okay. Sassy won't catch them. She never does," said Anna to her older sister.

"Ducks! Where are they?" barked Sassy. Sniffing the air, she barked, "I smell them!" And off she went as fast as she could, following the smell in the air.

"Let her chase as many of those wild ducks as she wants. She would be doing me a favor by running them off," said the grandfather as he was helping unload the truck.

Bark! Bark! "I see them!" *Bark! Bark!* Sassy was running as fast as she could toward the pond, where two ducks were enjoying their daily swim.

"Sam! That's not funny! I told you the next time you did that, I was going to bite you on your tail!" Fran said.

"That's not me barking like a dog! I thought it was you trying to be funny this time!" Just as Sam finished his sentence, there was a loud splash as Sassy jumped into the water.

"What was that?" Fran asked.

"It's just a dog, Fran, *Dog*!" Sam replied.

"I'm going to get you!" Sassy cried out.

"Fran! When was the last time we were chased by a dog?" Sam asked his wife with some laughter in his voice.

"Just last winter when we were down south," Fran answered.

Sam began to swim in front of Sassy, teasing her. "Dog, what makes you think you can catch me?" He said as he wiggled his tail feathers at Sassy. "You are all the same! You see a duck, and for some reason, you think you can catch us. I can't even begin to count the number of times one of you has jumped in the water thinking you are going to catch a duck. We are designed for the water. We glide on the water as graceful as a fish in the water. Just give it up. You've had your bath now, just leave."

Watching her husband from the sky above, Fran said, "Sam, stop getting so close to her!"

Getting a little too overconfident about teasing Sassy, Sam looked up at Fran. "She can't catch me!" he said as he slowed down so as to make Sassy think she had a chance. Just as he did, Sassy lunged forward. "*Ouch!*" Sam screamed as he took flight.

"I got one of your tail feathers! Next time, I will get more!" Sassy yelled happily, with Sam's tail feather in her mouth.

"Dog! Jesse is not going to be happy about what you did to my husband!" Fran yelled down to Sassy from above. "And you! I told you not to get so close to that dog! But no! Do you ever listen to me!" Fran was very upset with Sam as they flew out of sight of Sassy.

I need to find the others and show them my trophy, Sassy thought as she climbed out of the water and shook off her fur. She strolled off and thought out loud, *Jesse? What is Jesse? Must be some kind of duck! If it is a duck, I'll have more tail feathers to add to my collection!* With a big smile on her face, she went off to find the others.

CHAPTER 2

Jesse

With Sassy off chasing ducks and Cinnamon exploring her new home, Ding decided to take this moment and just enjoy his new yard by taking a nap under the shade of a walnut tree.

"Jack! You're supposed to be collecting food for the winter," Mary yelled down from the tree.

"I am!" Jack replied, quickly jumping back onto his feet. "I was just trying to take a break for a moment against this nice warm, furry rock."

"Furry rock? Rocks are not furry!" Mary said.

"Well, this one is! And come to think of it, I don't remember there being a rock here before?" So Jack began to investigate this strange-looking rock. As he walked around to the front of the rock, it began to move.

"Jack! That's no rock. It's a dog!" Mary yelled. "Get away from it before you wake it up!"

Jack quickly ran for the tree just as Ding was starting to wake up. "Who's making all that noise?" Ding asked with a yawn as he wiped the sleep from his eyes.

What is that? Ding thought out loud.

"Squirrel!" Ding loved chasing after squirrels; it's the best game ever. Off he ran after the squirrel, but he was not able to make it in time as Jack ran up the tree to the safety of a branch.

"Squirrel! Who are you calling a squirrel, you dumb dog!" Jack yelled from the safety of his tree as he looked down at Ding.

"Why, you! You are a squirrel, and I really enjoy chasing squirrels!" Ding said with a smile.

"I'm not a squirrel!" Jack angrily yelled at Ding. "I'm a chipmunk! And proud of it!"

"Ouch!" Ding cried out as he was struck in the head.

"That's for chasing my husband!" Mary yelled as she threw another walnut at Ding.

This time, Ding saw it coming and avoided the walnut, only to be struck from behind by the one Jack threw.

"Will you all please stop hitting me with acorns, please!" Ding yelled.

"You really are a dumb dog! You don't know the difference between a walnut and an acorn!" Jack said.

"Maybe not! But I do know that they hurt! And my name is not dog! It's Ding!" he said.

"Well, hello there, Ding. I'm Jack, and that lovely chipmunk over there is my wife, Mary," Jack answered. "If you want to chase a squirrel, you'll have to go to the next farm because you will not find any here! Now just so you know! Everything inside this fence is ours!" Jack said with a demanding voice.

"Yours! Well I now live here, so you are going to have to learn to be friendly with me," Ding answered. "And besides, there's only the two of you."

"So you think there are only two of us," Jack answered with a smile.

Ding did not like that smile and had a feeling he was going to regret his remarks about there only being two of them.

"Just so you know, Ding, in case you have any doubts about who's in charge!" Jack said with a grin. "Family, show him who's in charge!"

The tree branches began to shake all around Ding. As he looked around the trees, there were chipmunks on almost every branch. Each one of them was holding a walnut in their hands. And then it began.

"Fire!" Jack yelled.

Ding took off running toward the back of the house as walnuts came hurtling toward him. Some missed him, but most of them did not. Finally, as he rounded the back of the house and was out of range of the chipmunks, he saw Cinnamon running out of the house, and just to his left, he heard someone laughing. He stopped dead in his tracks. He couldn't believe what he was seeing. Ding had seen other dogs before that were taller than him, but he had never seen one this tall and laughing at him.

"Big dog! Big dog!" Cinnamon barked out loud as she ran toward the fence where it was standing. "I'm going to protect my family from you!"

As Cinnamon approached the big brown dog barking, it lowered its head over the fence and down to the ground and replied to Cinnamon, "Just who do you think you are calling a dog?" She asked, "Do I look like a dog to you?"

Cinnamon just stared in shock at how huge the head was on this dog. She did not know what to say.

"I am a horse. A quarter horse, to be more specific," she replied as she raised her head up from Cinnamon. "My name is Jesse."

"Mine is Ding," he replied as he approached the fence. "And my little friend here is Cinnamon." Ding sat there, just looking in amazement at the height of Jesse.

"Glad to meet you both," she replied. "I see you have been introduced to the chipmunk family that lives here on the farm," Jesse said with a smile. "Their aim is better than their bite."

"I have to agree with you on that," Ding replied, rubbing his head and back.

As Sassy came out of the tall grass from the pond, she saw her friends. She was so excited about her feather she didn't notice Jesse as she came around a tree. "Hey! Look at what I have!"

"That better not be a feather from the ducks that live by the pond!" Jesse said in a loud, demanding voice.

Sassy looked in the direction of the voice and then looked up. The feather fell from her lips as she looked in shock at the size of Jesse. Ding gave Sassy a nudge to bring her out of her state of shock.

"Feather? What feather? And what kind of dog are you?" Sassy asked.

"Hmmm! I am not a dog! I am a horse and the guardian of this farm and all those who call it home!" Jesse replied. "And that feather better be something you found!"

"Yes! Yes! I found it! I did not bite it off that duck!" Sassy answered quickly.

Jesse looked at Sassy with doubt in her face as she stared at her.

CHAPTER 3

Ding

"So, Ding? What kind of breed of dog are you? I know what breed of dog the other two are, but you, I've never seen you before," Jesse asked with a puzzled look.

"He's Ding! The dingy dingo!" Cinnamon answered quickly with excitement.

"Dingo! Hmm? Never heard of that breed before," said Jesse. "Where do you come from?"

"That truck!" Cinnamon answered quickly before Ding could speak.

"She was talking to Ding!" Sassy answered with a hateful look.

"Enough, you two! She meant where I was born," Ding replied. "I really don't know? I was out playing with my other brothers and sisters in the woods when a storm started one evening. We were following our mother back to our den. The sky grew dark, and the rain came down so hard that it hurt. I was the last one in line following my sister when something hit me in the head.

"When I woke up, the rain was gone, and it was nighttime. I did what my mother said and looked for her scent. But the rain had washed it away. I wandered around, trying to find my way home. I came across an opening in the woods, and the sky was lit up with little lights. They were so peaceful that I fell asleep.

"When I woke up the next day, I was so hungry. As I looked around, nothing looked familiar. I couldn't even find my own scent, so I could not go back the way I came.

"Then I smelled something. A new scent. I was so hungry that I followed it. It took me to a strange-looking bush.

"As I looked around it trying to find what the smell was, it moved. I started barking because I was not going to be scared by any bush that smelled good enough to eat.

"So I bit it, and the bush yelled out, 'Who's the dingy that bit me!' As the bush moved, it got taller. As it turned around, I saw a face.

"'Okay! Sergeant, you have been found.'

"'Only because something bit me in the butt!" the sergeant replied as he turned around to see me sitting on the ground. 'If it had not been for this little guy here, you would have walked right on by.'

"The bush was a human. My mother had talked to us pups about them, but she had never seen one before. She had told us that there was a time when the dingoes used to live with humans. We protected them, we hunted with them, and in return, they fed us and gave us a home.

"Maybe if I go with this human, he can help me find my way home.

"The sergeant reached down and picked me up, and immediately, I could smell that scent again. I wiggled loose from his grip and crawled inside of the bush. *I found it!* I thought as I barked out with joy.

"'Hey! You dingy little pup! Where do you think you are going!" the sergeant yelled out with laughter in his voice. 'You better not be digging into my lunch! That MRE is mine!'

"As the other soldiers began to gather around laughing, I was chewing on the sergeant's pack, trying to get the food.

"'Don't just stand there! Get this dingy puppy out of my pack!" the sergeant yelled out, laughing.

"The other soldiers began helping their sergeant out of his ghil-lie suit. In the meantime, I had managed to crawl inside of the sergeant's pack and was trying to eat his lunch. They pulled me out of the backpack with the sergeant's lunch still in my mouth.

"'Looks like he likes MREs better than you, sarge!' said one of the soldiers.

"Taking me into his lap, the sergeant said jokingly, 'You really have to be hungry to want to eat an MRE!'

"'Here, little guy, let me have that,' the sergeant said as he took the MRE from me.

"The sergeant opened the meal and began to look inside of it as I sat in his lap, hoping for something to eat. 'Well today is your lucky day, pup. This hot dog should fill your belly.'

"I, wasting no time, grabbed the hotdog and began eating it. *I don't know what kind of food this is, but I want more of it*, I thought.

"'So I wonder how he got out here?' one of the soldiers asked.

"'I doubt he belongs to anyone, but I will take him back with us and have the base veterinarian look at him,' replied the sergeant. 'Well, I guess you are going to need a name?' said the sergeant as he held me up to his face.

"'How about Ding!' one of the young privates yelled out.

"'Hmm! Well, young pup, what do you think of the name Ding?' the sergeant asked.

"I did not know at the time what the sergeant was talking about. All I knew was that I was still hungry, so I started barking, hoping he would give me another hot dog.

"The sergeant started giggling. 'Well I guess you like the name! So it's decided, then. Your name will be Ding!'

"As the sergeant set me down by his feet, I saw the package where the hot dog came from. I decided if he was not going to get it for me, then I would get it myself. Just as soon as he let go of me, I darted toward the package.

"'Hey, now, Ding! I still have to eat!' the sergeant said, laughing, as he reached down and picked up the MRE.

"'I have a hot dog that he can eat!' the young private said as he offered it to me.

"After I ate that second one, my tummy was full. And I was ready for a nap. So I curled up next to the sergeant and lay down.

"'Looks like someone is going to sleep?' said the sergeant as he reached down and picked me up. 'Here now, Ding, let's make you a bed in the Humvee.'

"The sergeant made me a little bed in the vehicle, and I curled up into the warm bed and fell asleep.

"I was awakened by the touch of a cold metal table. As I woke up and looked around the room, a man wearing a white shirt walked in.

"'Hello there, sergeant. My assistant tells me you found a puppy this morning during training,' said the captain as he walked into the room.

"'It's more like he found me when he took a bite out of me,' the sergeant said jokingly to the captain.

"'Well I don't think you tasted very good to him!' the captain said, laughing. 'So let's look him over and do a few tests to see how healthy he is.'

"So the man in the white suit shined a light in my eyes and stuck me with something sharp. *That hurts*, I thought as I growled at the man in the white shirt.

"'He did not like that,' the sergeant said. 'What breed of dog do you think he is?'

"'Good question? I'm not sure! But I am sure I can find out for you,' the captain replied.

"The man in white left. I was getting cold on that table, so the sergeant found me a blanket to lie on.

"The door opened up. 'I don't see his breed in any of my books, so if you don't mind, I would like to take a picture of Ding and send it to a friend of mine, who's very good at identifying breeds of dogs when they are still a puppy,' the captain asked.

"'Yes, please. I would really like to know,' the sergeant said.

"There were a lot of strange smells in the air that I had no idea what they were. But the sounds of other dogs, and at the time I didn't know it was the sound of cats, really had me puzzled as to what could be making the sound. As I lay there listening to all the different sounds around me and wondering what they could be, the man in the white shirt came back in.

"'Well all the tests came back good, and my friend knew the breed of your puppy. He's an American dingo, also known as the American Indian dog, a breed that was believed extinct at one time. You found yourself a very rare breed of dog,' the captain said.

"The sergeant looked at Ding, chuckling. 'Guess when I called you a dingy pup, I was not too far-off from the name of your breed. So naming you Ding is a good name for you.' Then he pet me on the head.

"So I stayed with the sergeant. Much time went by, and I got bigger. But I never forgot about my family. Every time we would go out, I would see new sights and hear new sounds and smell the smells in the air. Some smells I knew, some were new, and others were so bad I wish I had not stuck my nose near it. But I was always searching for the scent of my mother.

"As time went on, the sergeant met a woman. I liked the way she smelled. Her scent reminded me of a field of wildflowers. She had two daughters, who would always give me hugs when they would come to visit."

CHAPTER 4

The Scent

"One day, they came to visit, and they brought Sassy and Cinnamon. This was the first time I was introduced to them. They were bickering as they got out of the car, and they still argue today."

"That's because I'm always right, and she's not!" Cinnamon spoke quickly, interrupting Ding's story.

"Shut up! You are always thinking you are in charge!" Sassy answered with an angry voice.

"Enough!" Jesse said, snorting at them.

"I am in charge!" Cinnamon said as she got a stern look from Sassy and Jesse.

"If you two are done, I would like to hear the rest of the story, please!" Jesse said as she looked at both Cinnamon and Sassy.

Ding, looking at Cinnamon, said, "So as I was saying! It was the first time I met Cinnamon and Sassy. And I thought how they reminded me of hearing my mother breaking up the arguments between us pups. The two of them were arguing so much that they walked right past me. They did not acknowledge me until I told them to stop arguing. Boy, was that a mistake.

"'Who do you think you are, telling me what to do!' Sassy answered in an angry voice.

"'Yeah! Who do you think you are!' Cinnamon answered as she quickly ran behind Sassy, trembling in fear.

"'I'm Ding,' I answered them.

"'Well, Ding? Let's get something straight! You don't interrupt me, ever!' Sassy answered, snarling.

"'Sassy!' the youngest daughter, Anna, hollered at her. 'You behave yourself right now!'

"'You're lucky my owner is coming to your rescue!' snarled Sassy.

"'Yeah! Lucky!' Cinnamon yelled out as she took off running to the house.

"'Ding! Sassy! You two need to get along!' the sergeant yelled as he came out of the house.

"Not wanting to cause any more problems, I went off to lie down under a tree as Sassy and Cinnamon both went into the house.

"When I was awoken later by the sergeant, it was time to go. We all climbed into the sergeant's truck. I rode in the bed of the truck this time since it was a little crowded inside the cab of the truck. But that was okay because I had a nice, cozy bed back there.

"That was when I saw her lying in my bed. 'Sassy, if you don't mind, I would like to have my bed,' I said as politely as I could.

"'Oh! This bed! This nice, cozy bed! I don't think so!' Sassy replied with a grin on her face.

"I was okay with riding in the bed of the truck. It didn't even bother me that she was rude to me earlier. But I was not going to be pushed out of my bed! 'That's my bed, and you will get out of it! *Now!*' I yelled at Sassy.

"'Let's get something straight!' Sassy replied with anger in her voice as she stood up and circled around me. 'No one! And I mean no one! Is going to tell me what to do!'

"I turned and faced her with a growl in my voice. 'Well you better get used to me telling you then!'

"Sassy jumped into the air. As she came to try and grab me, I lunged my head into her chest and knocked the wind out of her. As she lay there gasping for air, I went and claimed my bed. 'As I told you! This is mine!'

"'Well I see that you two have finally worked out your friendship. Sassy, I suggest you don't challenge Ding anymore, so go find you a spot and lie down,' the sergeant said.

"Sassy went and found a spot next to me. 'I'm sorry,' she said to me. Sassy had learned that day that her days of being a bully were over. Her and Cinnamon still argue like sisters, but she is not a bully anymore.

"When the truck stopped, I looked out over the bed of the truck and thought that this place looked familiar. 'I know this place!'

"Waking from her nap, Sassy asked with a yawn, 'What do you mean you know this? What are you talking about?' Sassy stood up, looking around. 'It's just a park. Unless there are ducks to chase, it's not going to be a fun place to visit.'

"'This is where I first met him, the sergeant,' Ding replied. 'I was lost and hungry when I found him pretending to be a bush.'

"'Why was he pretending to be a bush?' Sassy asked with a puzzled look.

"'I don't know? Why do these humans do strange things?' Ding answered with a smile.

"'Come on, you two, it's time to get out of the truck,' hollered the sergeant. Looking at the mother of the daughters, "Wendy, this is the place I was telling you about. This is where I found Ding, or he found me,' the sergeant said with a grin.

"'Found Ding? I thought you picked him up from a shelter?' the youngest daughter, Annie, asked.

"'No, I met Ding here during a military training exercise. Come on and I will tell you and your sister Chey the story of how Ding and I met during lunch,' exclaimed the sergeant.

"As they sat there eating their lunch and the sergeant was telling them how I took a bite out of him, I could smell something in the air. I was not sure what it was, but I was curious enough to go and find it.

"'Ding, where are you going?' Sassy asked.

"'I'm going to find out what that scent is,' Ding replied. 'Do you want to come?'

"'Yes! Anything is better than lying here and listening to them,' Sassy replied.

"'I'm coming too. Someone has to be in charge of you two, and that's me!' Cinnamon said in her commanding voice.

"'I should have eaten you when you were a puppy!' Sassy said in an angry voice with a smile of delight on her face.

"'Do you two ever stop bickering?' Ding asked.

"'*No!*' Cinnamon and Sassy said together.

"As I followed the scent in the air, I thought, *I know this scent, but I just can't place it.* Everything I had ever smelled was running through my head, but I just couldn't put a paw on it.

"As the grass grew taller, Cinnamon and Sassy began to worry. They were not the explorer that I was.

"'I think we should turn around, Ding!' Cinnamon spoke out with a frightened voice.

"'I'm with her. I think we have gone too far from our owners!' Sassy said, trying not to show any fear.

"'You two can wait here if you like, but I have to find this scent. I have to know what it is!' I told them.

"So Sassy and Cinnamon sat there in grass tall enough that Cinnamon could barely see over it, waiting for me to return.

"'The scent has moved down to the ground. Now I can follow it much better, Sassy!' I said out loud. Then I remembered that they had stayed behind, waiting for me to return.

"As I continued to follow the scent, I discovered a second one that was right beside the first one. The second scent was similar to the first one but different.

"*I'm beginning to wonder if I'm being hunted. Well, if I am, I better find them first*, I thought. As I followed the scent, it split up. 'The scent is going in two different directions, one to the left and the other one is—oh no!' I just realized it was not me that they were hunting. It was Cinnamon and Sassy.

"'I'm getting scared. I want to go back. Do you know how to get back?' the scared little Cinnamon asked Sassy.

"'Of course, I do! We came this way, or was it that way?' Sassy was just as scared as Cinnamon but was trying not to show it. 'We are going to be okay. Before you know it, Ding will be back.'

"Just then, Cinnamon and Sassy heard something coming toward them.

"'See, there he comes now,' Sassy calmly said to Cinnamon. 'Ding, we are still waiting on you!' she said out loud. After speaking out, the sound just stopped. 'Ding! Stop trying to scare us! We know it's you!' Sassy said in a demanding voice.

"'I don't think it's him, Sassy,' Cinnamon whispered to Sassy.

"'I think you're right!' Sassy replied quietly to Cinnamon.

"As they sat there wondering what was going to come out of the high grass, 'Ding! If you don't come out and stop trying to scare us, then I will come in and get you!' Sassy yelled, trying to build up enough courage just to be able to move. 'That's it! Here I come!' Sassy slowly started moving toward what she thought was Ding trying to play a trick on them.

"With Cinnamon staying close to Sassy as she moved toward where the rustling in the high grass came from, they heard another sound just to their left.

"'What's that noise?' the scared little Cinnamon asked.

"Before Sassy could answer what had been making the first sound in front of them, all of a sudden, another dog leaped out of the tall grass at them. As Sassy fell backward onto Cinnamon, she yelled in fear, 'That's not Ding!'

"I, leaping out of the high grass, landed on the back of the attacker. Grabbing the attacker by the neck, I whipped my body over the top of the attacker and threw the attacker into the air and onto their back.

"Cinnamon, crawling out from under Sassy, said, 'Who is that? She looks like Ding!'

"After hitting the ground hard on their back, the attacker started to stand up. 'This is my kill! You are trespassing in my territory!' the attacker told me in an angry voice.

"'We meant no intrusion! These are my friends! We are just here with our humans visiting!' I replied, trying to convince the attacker we meant no harm.

"'Dingoes do not live with humans anymore. We have not lived with them for years!' the attacker talked as she circled around me. 'You look like a dingo, but you can't be one! Dingoes don't live in human packs anymore, nor do they live with prey!'

"'Well, this one does!' I growled at the attacker. 'I don't want to fight you! We just want to leave!'

"'You are not going to just trespass onto my pack's land and expect to just leave without a fight!' the attacker growled back at me.

"'Stop!' A voice came from behind Sassy and Cinnamon.

"As everyone turned to see who was speaking, there stood another dingo. 'We will let you leave peacefully, but first, you have to tell me how you came to live with a human pack?'

"'Sassy! Cinnamon! Ding!' was being heard in the distance behind the second dingo.

"The second dingo looked at my friends. 'You two may go!' Looking at me, the second dingo asked, 'You, will stay and answer the question?'

"Sassy and Cinnamon looked at me on what to do. 'It's okay, just follow the voice of your owners to get back.'

"As they ran off toward the voices of their owners, Sassy looked back one last time before disappearing into the distance.

"As they left, I began to tell the story of how I had gotten lost from my pack and was now living with humans. As I told my story, the other two dingoes' eyes began to tear up.

"The dingo I was fighting with tackled me, saying, 'Brother!'

"With a surprisingly puzzled look, I replied, 'Sian!'

"'Runty! You are finally home!' Sian barked happily to me.

"As I stood back up with a smile on my face and my sister by my side, I noticed that there were more dingoes gathering around me. With a tear in my eye, I approached the second dingo. 'Mother?'

"'Yes, son, you are home!' she replied with a smile. 'I thought I would never find my little pup again. The entire pack searched for days, trying to find you. And here you are! My little pup is all grown up!'

"'Ding! Ding! Where are you!' I could hear the sergeant calling for me.

"The other dingoes disappeared back into the high grass.

"'So they call you Ding. That is a very good name for you. It was the name of my grandfather who was a great pack leader. And he too was the runt in the litter of pups,' my mother told me. 'You are already bringing honor to the name when you stood up to your sister to protect your pack. I'm sure you will be as good of a pack leader as he was.'

"'There you are, Ding!' the sergeant said with a sigh of relief. 'Should have known that you would be out here making new friends.' With no fear in him, the sergeant walked right up to my mother and sat down between the two of us.

"'I see your friend has no fear in him like you, son,' she spoke to me. 'But what is that delicious smell on him?'

"'The smell is called a hot dog!' I laughed as I replied, 'It's one of my favorite things to eat!'

"Licking me on the nose, my mother said, 'I have to go, son, and so do you. Your pack needs you.' Just before she disappeared into the high grass, she turned and looked at me. 'I love you, and I will always be with you!'

"Looking at me, 'This must be where you came from, and I'm guessing that was your mother!' said the sergeant, petting me on the head. "Well, it's time to go, and the others are probably wondering where we are?' Following the sergeant, the two of us headed back to meet up with the others.

"When we returned, the three ladies had already put everything back in the bed of the truck. While the sergeant told them what he had seen when he found me, I climbed into the bed of the truck and searched for a package of hot dogs in the cooler. I wanted to share the delicious food with my mother.

"I jumped out of the back of the truck and went back in the direction I had come from and placed the hot dog package on the ground. Then I howled to let my mother know I had left her a present.

"'Come on, Ding, it's time to go!' the sergeant called out to me.

"I jumped back into the bed of the truck and was greeted by Sassy and Cinnamon, who had jumped through the back window of the cab.

"'Tell us? What happened when we left?' barked the overzealous Cinnamon. 'I was about to come and save you! I was going to bite those two mean dogs on the tail!'

"'You! Bite someone! You're scared of your own shadow!' Sassy said, laughing out loud.

"'I'm sure you would have been too much for them to handle, Cinnamon,' I said, trying to be friendly and not laugh. 'Now if you just let me get comfortable, I will tell you both.'

"As I started to lie down, I heard my mother's howl. I looked out the bed of the truck to see her and the others all enjoying their first taste of hot dogs. As we drove away, I told Sassy and Cinnamon that they were my family I had been looking for."

CHAPTER 5

Scout

With tears in her eyes, Jesse lowered her head to Ding. "Your story reminds me of my mother, who passed away fifteen years ago. I'm sorry you didn't get to know your family longer, but I am sure they are happy to know you are safe and around friends and family."

Scratching her head, "If you don't mind me asking, just how old are you?" Sassy asked.

"I will be thirty years old this winter," Jesse replied. "Like my mother, I was born here on this farm."

"All right, you three, it's time to come in." They turned around to see Wendy standing in the back door, motioning for them to come.

"It is getting late. I guess we will see you tomorrow, Jesse," Ding said as he turned to head to the house.

Jesse nodded as she headed to her feed trough for she knew it would not be long before they came to feed her.

As Jesse approached her feed trough, a frightened little fox stepped out from behind a tree. "You know you are not allowed in this part of the farm!" Jesse spoke with anger in her voice. "You better have a good reason to be here before I kick you over the fence again!"

Rubbing his rear, remembering the day she did that to him for trying to steal duck eggs, the fox said, "I…I…I was sent here again… again…against my will to let you know that he is at the meeting place. Now ple-ple-please let me leave peacefully."

"You may go!" Jesse answered, snorting at the scared little fox.

Jesse turned around and headed to the back of the farm. As she reached the back fence behind the trees, she could smell him. "Scout! You coward, you can't hide that stench of your kind in the cornfield!" she bellered out, stomping at the ground.

"Jesse, you always say the nicest things to me," Scout said as he stepped out of the cornfield with his two cohorts on each side of him.

"Hay, Scout, I don't think she meant it as a compliment!" said the skinny coyote known as Bones.

Scout, raising his right paw, turned to Bones, but instead of hitting him, he smacked Tails, the smallest of the three, causing Tails to drop the mouse he was snacking on.

Tails never got very tall like the rest of the coyotes, but his tail did. His tail was so long he could completely wrap it around himself. "What did you hit me for?" Tails asked.

Raising his paw again, "Do you really want me to give you an answer!" Scout said in his demanding voice.

Knowing better than to answer, Tails jumped at Bones, yelling, "Give me back my mouse!"

Bones took off into the cornfield, chomping on the mouse, with Tails chasing him, trying to get it back.

"Now that they are gone," Scout said as he turned back around to face Jesse with a smile on his face, "I see you have some new friends moving in today."

Jesse rushed the fence. Scout turned and ran into the cornfield in fear of Jesse. Scout was just about to disappear into the field when he remembered that there was an electric fence between them.

"I see you still have the yellow stripe running down your back!" Jesse said with a grin.

"Ha ha ha!" Scout replied as he came back out of the cornfield. "I see you still have a sense of humor for being as old as you are. Let's see now, you should be about, what, thirty years old by now. It has to be getting hard for you to make your daily patrols around the farm on those old bones of yours."

"All you have to do is come across the fence and find out how strong these old bones are," Jesse answered as she stood there, showing no fear of Scout.

"I'd love nothing more than to come over and take a nibble on you!" he replied as he took a lunge at the fence, trying to scare Jesse, but she did not even flinch. "But I don't want to be the one who breaks the truce you have with the chief. But if you ever want to take a stroll out into the cornfield, I would be more than happy to share you with the others," Scout said, smiling at Jesse.

"Ohh! That's right! You are not an alpha, are you? You are still having to take orders the same way your family has for years!" Jesse answered with a smirk.

"Leave my family out of this conversation!" Scout didn't like it when he was reminded that his family had never been looked upon as an alpha in his pack. "The chief is getting old, and just like you, his days are numbered. And when I become the new alpha, there will no longer be a truce for you to hide behind."

Jesse turned away from Scout, heading back to eat. "Well? I only chat with the alphas of the pack, so goodbye, beta!"

"I'm not a beta!" Getting red in the face, Scout yelled at her, "Jesse, you get back here! I did not say we were done! Jesse!" But she just kept on going, disappearing into the woods that surrounded the farm.

Still sitting there, Scout grew madder by the minute. "How dare that horse call me a beta! The rest of the pack may treat me as a beta! But she will show me respect for I am an *alpha*! *Do you hear me, Jesse! I am an alpha!*" Scout yelled as loud as he could.

Walking back to meet up with their brother Scout, Tails and Bones could hear him yelling, and they both knew that when he got angry, the safest thing to do was to stay away. Without saying a word to each other, they turned around and started heading home.

Scout jumped out in front of his brothers. "Where have you two been?" he asked, showing his fangs and growling in anger.

Tails, too scared to talk, looked at Bones for the answer. Bones, thinking really hard, replied, "Uhh, is this a trick question?"

Scout raised his paw, ready to hit Bones, when he got interrupted by the howl of another coyote calling for the pack to return home. Putting down his paw, Scout turned to head home. "Let's go!" he said in a grumpy voice.

As Ding, Sassy, and Cinnamon lay on the floor, watching television with the family, they too could hear the howl of the coyote.

Bark! Bark! Bark! Cinnamon ran to the window behind the TV.

"Your Chihuahua thinks she's going to protect us from the coyotes!" the sergeant said to Wendy, laughing.

Wendy called her Chihuahua to her, and Cinnamon jumped into her lap. "Yes! You scared off the coyotes for me," she said while petting her.

As Wendy and the sergeant continued to joke with each other, Sassy looked to Ding who was lying beside her. "What was that howl? I've never heard anything like it before, and I don't think I want to meet the dog it came from either!"

Ding, raising his head, said, "I was sleeping until Cinnamon started barking."

"So you didn't hear that howl?" Sassy was really hoping he knew what it was.

"No. But we can ask Jesse tomorrow what it was," Ding answered, hoping to just go back to sleep.

As Scout and his brothers returned home, the alphas were just getting done chewing on a deer they had killed. As the alphas followed the leader of the pack off to the nightly meeting they had, Scout grabbed a leg from the kill and went off to where he could watch the meeting and wondered what they were talking about.

"Does anyone have anything to report tonight?" asked the chief as he looked around at the four alphas' council members.

"I do, Dad!" Snow stepped out from behind her father. Snow was his daughter and only child. Her coat was as white as snow, and with her light-blue eyes, all the alpha males were asking for her hand in marriage.

"Snow, you know that the females are not allowed to be in the meeting!" the chief said, trying to be stern with his daughter.

"I know," Snow said as she walked into the middle of the circle of alphas, "but a new family moved into the old farmhouse, and besides, I didn't hear anyone else say anything about it!"

"Well, does anyone know anything about the new family that moved in today?" the chief asked the other alphas.

"I know someone who saw them, Father! Scout witnessed them moving in!" Snow was the only friend Scout had in the alphas. They had known each other since they were puppies. Even though Snow's mother was an alpha and Scout's mom was a beta, the two of them were best friends, and they would let their puppies play together. Snow's father never liked to see alpha and beta puppies playing together, but he was never going to tell her mother what she could do.

"So someone bring me Scout, and you, young lady, need to leave. I will talk with you later." The chief noticed that everyone was staring at his daughter as she walked away. "If you all are done, will you bring me Scout!"

As the alphas scrambled to get their brains working again, one of them finally managed to call for Scout.

Scout, lying there and gnawing at his bone, couldn't believe that he was being called to the meeting. Only the head alphas and the chief were ever allowed to attend the meeting. As the alpha called for Scout again, Bones went over to his brother and smacked him on his head. "They are calling you!"

Scout, rubbing his head, said, "Yeah, yeah! You're right, I better get going!" He was so nervous to be going to the meeting he did not do or say anything to Bones about hitting him.

"I can't believe you hit him!" Tails was more excited about one of them finally doing what they both have been wanting to do since they were puppies. "How did it feel?"

It took a minute before Bones realized what Tails was asking him. As he sat there thinking about it, he began to smile. The smile didn't last because at that very same moment, Bones noticed that Scout had left the deer leg behind, and all he could think about was how good it would taste. "Good!" he said as he reached out to pick up the deer leg.

As Scout approached the meeting, the other elder alphas stepped to the side to let him enter the center of the circle. As he stepped into the circle, he tried to calm himself. "I am Scout!" He could hear the fear in his voice and hoped that it was not noticeable.

The chief, looking upon Scout, noticed that he was afraid to be standing there in the center among the alphas. "It's okay to be a little nervous, young pup. You are probably wondering why you are here?"

Unable to get his voice to work, Scout just nodded.

"I was told that you saw the new family that moved in today?" the chief tried to ask without making Scout any more nervous than he was.

"Umm, yes! Yes! I did see them move into the old farmhouse." Scout did his best to speak before the chief.

The chief walked over to Scout and sat down next to him. "There is no reason to be nervous. But I would like to know what it is you saw today?"

Scout, trying to build up confidence, sat up straight. "It was a man and woman with two children and three house dogs. One was a Chihuahua, the other was an Australian shepherd, but the third one, I have never seen before. I tried to have that stubborn old horse tell me, but she wouldn't!"

"She is stubborn, ain't she!" the chief responded with a giggle. "I remember when I was a young pup, and my father was the chief. He warned me about Jesse and to never go hunting on her land. But I was not going to be intimidated by any horse, nor was I going to not hunt where I wanted to hunt.

"So I sneaked away that day and crawled through the fence into her land. I was sure that no one had seen me. I made my way up to where the farmer kept his chickens. I was lucky that day. Not only were the chickens outside of the coop but I was also going to prove to my father that I was not scared of a horse, and I was going to bring home a chicken too.

"As I sneaked closer to my prey, I got this uneasy feeling that I was not alone. Then I heard a voice. 'I hope you are just here to visit, young pup?' There she stood right above me. The only thing I could think of was to run. So I did, ran as fast as I could for the fence, and I made it. At least so I thought. I was so scared that I imagined running for safety. I did not come out of my dream until I heard my father's voice as Jesse sat me down right in front of him.

"'Young pup, just what do you think you are doing?' I was more scared of my father than that horse. 'Thank you for bringing me my son. I believe he has learned his lesson about trespassing!'

"Jesse lowered her head and whispered into my ear, 'Try and look brave in front of your father!' She smiled at my father and walked away.

"I tried to look as brave as I could, like she told me. 'I know we are not supposed to go hunting on her land, but I wanted to prove that I was not scared of that horse.'

"He didn't say a word. He just turned around and started walking home. Now I was really scared as I followed my father home. I kept waiting for him to say something, anything. The silence was killing me.

"Once we arrived at the den, he looked over his shoulder, smiling at me, and said, 'I'll let you tell your mother!'

"I knew then I had nothing to prove to my father, and he was proud of me no matter what." Giggling, the chief said, "But having to face my mother, I would rather go back and face that horse again."

"Yeah, my mom was scary too!" Scout said with a smile.

The chief, returning back to the head of the circle, turned to counsel of alphas. "I think it's time to let this young coyote join the other young coyotes in training?"

Scout did not know what to say or do as the alphas looked upon him and at one another. As he continued to look around, one by one, all the alphas began to howl.

The chief smiled at Scout. "Then it's agreed that you Scout will join the hunting party and begin your training."

As the alphas dispersed, Scout was still sitting there, smiling, and thinking how he had gone from being a beta to an alpha.

As Snow walked up to Scout and teasingly brushed against him, she said, "You could at least say hello."

"Yes! Yes! Hello, Snow!" Scout replied as he realized he was no longer alone.

As Snow continued to walk around Scout, smiling, she said, "So I hear you are going to join the young coyotes in learning how to hunt? And then the dream you have had since we were puppies will come true."

As Scout remembered how he told everyone that someday he would be an alpha, he began to grin. "Yes! And I also said I would be the head alpha, you would be my wife, and I would allow the pack to hunt on Jesse's land!"

With a little attitude in her voice, Snow asked, "Do you really think I would marry you?" As Snow got face-to-face with Scout, she said, "And to hunt on her land, you would have to get approval from the council of alphas!"

Running toward their brother full of joy about the news, they tackled him. "We heard the news! You are going to be an alpha!" yelled Tails as he stood on his brother's chest.

"I think you boys better not celebrate too much!" Snow told them as she walked away. "Because I'm sure you have not forgotten that tomorrow the pack moves to the winter hunting grounds."

"Get off me!" snarled Scout. "Let's go!" He said as he led his brothers back to their den. He thought, *If I was in charge, things would be different!*

CHAPTER 6

Passing the Torch

The next morning, Ding, Sassy, and Cinnamon were lying in the shade of the old apple tree, watching their family making repairs to the corral fence, when Jesse came walking up to them.

"I was hoping to see you today," Ding said as he stood up to greet Jesse. "We were hoping that you might be able to tell us what was all the howling last night?"

"Those were coyotes!" Jesse answered. "And by the look on your faces, I'm guessing you have never heard of them?"

As the three of them looked at one another, Sassy was the first to speak. "No, we haven't!"

"They are wild and very cunning dogs that hunt in a pack." As Jesse stood there explaining, Ding was fascinated how the coyote family reminded him of his. "The howling you heard is how they communicate to one another."

"What do they hunt!" Sassy asked.

Jesse lowered her head. "Whatever they can catch!" Turning her head to Cinnamon, she said, "Especially little dogs!"

That was enough to scare Cinnamon. "No! They will never get me!" she yelled as she took off running to the house.

"I don't know what is going on over there, Wendy, but I think Jesse just scared Cinnamon!" the sergeant said jokingly to his wife.

"She probably did something to her!" Wendy replied, laughing.

"Have they ever been on the farm?" Sassy asked with hope that the answer would be no.

Seeing the fear in Sassy's eyes, Jesse answered, "Yes, they have. But I run them off before they could do any harm. There is supposed to be a truce between us."

"What's this truce you have?" Ding wanted to know.

"It's more of an agreement." Both dogs listened closely as Jesse spoke. "If they stay on the other side of the fence, then I won't kick them back over it!"

Both Ding and Sassy started laughing. "That would stop me from getting near you!" replied Ding. "But does it really work?"

With a big smile on her face, Jesse answered, "Yes! For the most part. Sometimes, a young pup wants to prove himself and would come on the farm, but I catch them every time!" With a more serious look, she said, "Which brings me to why I am here today. I'm getting too old to be chasing off these coyotes, and they know it. A day will come, Ding, when it will be up to you to chase off the predators!"

"I would be honored to help you!" Ding answered as he stood up.

"The leaves are falling, and the coyotes will be leaving for better hunting grounds. They will not return until spring, so you have time to learn the layout of the farm." As Jesse turned around, she said, "If you would come with me, I will show you the boundaries of the farm."

"That sounds like work. I think I will just stay here and nap," Sassy said as she yawned and lowered her head. Ding left with Jesse to become more familiar with the farm.

"I never knew it would be this big!" Ding said as he sat next to the grain bins, talking with Jesse. He was still amazed about just how big the farm was and how the wooded area of the farm reminded him of his childhood.

As the leaves fell from the trees around Jesse, she closed her eyes. "I'm going to miss this time of the year most of all. This is going to be my last winter."

"Last winter?" Ding, looking up at Jesse, was puzzled about her comment. "What are you talking about?"

"I will be joining my mother soon." Thinking of seeing her mother again brought a smile to Jesse. "You have until spring to prepare yourself for the return of the coyotes. Once they learn I am gone, they will start coming onto the land again to hunt. You must be ready!"

"I will be ready!" Ding was still puzzled. "Where do horses go?"

Jesse smiled, remembering what her mother had told her. "The soul of an animal goes to a land where predator and prey live together in peace."

Saddened by the thought of losing Jesse so soon, Ding looked at her. "I promise to learn everything from you so I will be ready when the coyotes return!"

Every day, Ding went exploring the farm and spending time with his friend Jesse. Ding would practice his stealth and tracking techniques by following Jesse's scent around the farm. Ding had improved his technique enough to be able to sneak up on Jesse without her knowing he was near.

As the days got shorter and the snow began to fall, his friend Jesse grew weaker.

"I'm glad you are going to be here when I leave," Jesse said, smiling at Ding with a tired look on her face. "I just need to lie down and rest for a bit," she said as she lowered herself down onto the bedding in her stall. "My mother is going to be shocked when I tell her I made a good friend with a dog!" she said with a giggle.

Ding lay down next to her, knowing that it was time. "I'm going to miss you, old friend."

Wendy and the girls came into the barn; they saw Ding and Jesse lying together. Wendy knew what was happening, and the three of them gathered around Jesse to say their goodbyes. Jesse laid her head on Wendy's lap and drifted off. The next day, the family buried Jesse next to her mother.

Ding never forgot his promise to Jesse. He continued to patrol the farm.

As he was out one day practicing, he came across a new scent. As he followed it, he was finding it difficult to step quietly in the deep snow. As he closed in on the scent, he heard a sound and knew immediately that what he was following was now coming toward him. Ding lay down in the snow, remembering how the chipmunks thought he was a rock and hoping it would work again.

As he lay there motionless, a little red fox came toward him. The little red fox stopped just a few feet in front of Ding and began sniffing the air and ground. Ding wondered if the fox knew he was there.

Once the little fox felt safe, he continued on his way. Ding followed the little fox, being careful not to let the little fox know he was behind him. Ding watched as the little fox crawled back through a hole that ran under the fence.

This little fox is just what I need to help me improve myself! Ding thought. So every day, he went out into the woods and followed the fox.

CHAPTER 7

Ding Makes a New Friend

As the snow began to melt and the days got warmer, Ding was out in the woods trying to find the scent of the little fox he had been following all winter. After a while, Ding decided he was going to take a nap. He curled up next to a tree and fell asleep to the warmth of the afternoon sun.

When he awoke, he sat up and stretched out and began sniffing the air to find the fox. "He smells really close!" He sniffed some more. "He's really close!" Just then, Ding felt something moving behind him. The little fox had fallen asleep behind him. Ding turned around and put a paw on him and asked in a calm voice, "It's time to wake up!"

The little fox opened his eyes and looked up at Ding. "Just a few more minutes, Dad!" He said then put his head back down and fell asleep.

A little shocked by what the fox said, Ding remembered what his mother used to do to wake him up! Ding took a deep breath and barked, "*Woof!*"

The little fox jumped to his feet! "O-o-okay! I'm…I'm awake!" Wiping the sleep from his eyes, the fox said, "I was getting…getting up, Dad!"

Ding started giggling at the little fox!

As the little fox's eyes begin to focus, he said, "You! You! You are not my dad!"

The little fox quickly turned around to run away. Ding just barely grabbed ahold of the little fox's tail. "I'm not going to hurt you!" he said, holding on to his tail. "I just want to talk!"

The little fox stopped trying to get away. "Do you promise not to tell Jesse too?"

Ding let go of the tail. "Yes! I will not tell her! Now my name is Ding," he said as he sat down.

"My name…name is Gus!" the frightened little fox replied. "You…you are not going to…to make fun of my…my…my stuttering, are you?"

"No! But I have never heard anyone talk that way either," Ding answered, wanting to know more. "Why do you talk that way?"

"I always have," Gus answered as he grew more relaxed that Ding was not going to hurt him or make fun of him. "My…my father talked the same way!"

Ding was still puzzled. "Your stuttering is getting better!"

"The calmer I get…get, the better it is!" Gus answered with a smile. "I have not seen Jesse all winter…winter, is she okay?"

"Are you friends with her?" Ding asked.

"Yes and no!" Gus answered, lowering his head. "I'm allowed to come into the woods and hunt mice but only the woods. I have not seen her all winter!"

Ding wondered why Jesse never told him about Gus. "Come with me, I need to show you something!" Ding led the way with Gus following close behind him. Ding stopped at the edge of the woods and pointed to where Jesse was buried next to her mother.

Gus began to cry. "With her…her gone, we are not safe! She was the only one…one the coyotes were afraid of!"

Trying to comfort Gus, Ding told him the promise he made. "I made a promise to Jesse that I would continue to safeguard the farm as she did."

As Sassy came out of the house, she went over to Ding and Gus. "Hey, Ding! Is this the fox you've been talking about!"

Gus didn't quite understand what she was talking about but had an idea. "It's…it's…it's been you! All win…win…winter! I thought som…someone was following me!"

"Yes, I was following you!" Ding said, trying to calm Gus down. "With Jesse gone, I needed someone to practice with."

"The coyotes are not going to…to fear a farm dog!" Gus was really getting excited about Jesse being gone and no one around to scare off the coyotes.

"Hey, now, Gus!" Sassy was a little upset with the little fox having no faith in Ding. "If anyone can scare off a coyote, it's going to be him!"

"All right, let's have everyone calm down!" Ding said, doing his best. "It's true I am not as tall or as strong as Jesse, but I will do my best to keep the coyotes away. You can continue to hunt mice in the woods. But I need you to let me know when the coyotes have returned. And don't tell them that Jesse is no longer here."

Gus was so scared of the coyotes he could barely speak. "You! You! You will know they are back when you hear the howl of the coyotes!" Gus turned around and ran into the woods.

"That's one scared little fox!" Sassy said, giggling.

Just before Ding walked away, he turned to Sassy with a look of seriousness. "We should all be!"

CHAPTER 8

Charles and Jane Arrive

As the trees began to show signs of the return of spring, the sergeant came pulling a trailer up to the corral. Wendy and the girls came running out of the house with all three dogs following them. All three dogs could hear a strange and unfamiliar sound coming from the trailer as they got closer.

"What do you think he has in there, Ding?" Sassy asked as they all approached the back of the trailer. Ding had no answer; he was just as curious as her.

"Come on, Dad! Open the door, please?" the impatient daughters asked. "We want to see them!"

As the door opened, the three dogs finally could see what was in the trailer. There, lying down in a bed of straw, in the nose of the trailer, were two small goats.

"Ah! They are so cute!" Wendy said as she went into the trailer with the girls. "Do they have names?"

"Yes, the buck is Charles, and the doe is Jane," the sergeant answered. "These two Boer goats are both three months old, but by December, they will be old enough to breed."

Wendy motioned to her daughters. "Come on, girls, let's get them out of the trailer and into the corral."

"I'll go get some bedding and a bale of hay for them." As the sergeant walked away, he called for the dogs to follow him. "Come on, you three, I don't want you to spook the goats as they come off the trailer."

Wendy and the girls took the two young goats into the barn while the sergeant tossed down a bale of hay and bedding from above.

Once the goats were all settled in, the three dogs went down to the corral to introduce themselves to the new members of the farm. The two young goats were busy playing and exploring their new surroundings.

"Hello and welcome to the farm!" Ding yelled to the two goats, trying to get their attention.

Charles ran over first, followed by Jane. "Hello, I'm Charles, and this is my friend Jane."

Trying to establish her dominance over the goats, Cinnamon said, "I'm Cinnamon, and I'm in charge!"

"This again! Do your ears ever get tired of hearing yourself talk?" replied Sassy as she stared at Cinnamon.

This made both goats start laughing.

"You two are funny!" replied Jane.

Ding tried to take control of the conservation before Sassy and Cinnamon could have a chance to argue. "She has already introduced herself. I am Ding, and this is Sassy."

Wendy and the sergeant approached the group. "Well, I'm glad to see you all are making friends," said the sergeant as he reached down to pet Ding and Sassy. "I'm going to need all three of you to help us keep an eye on these goats."

As Wendy and the sergeant went into the corral to play with the goats, Ding was wondering how much more time he had before the coyotes returned.

Sassy could see that Ding was worrying and gave him a nudge. "Everything is going to be okay! Remember, you are not alone in this! You also have us and the rest of the family to help you. And if any dog could scare off the coyotes, it's definitely you!"

Cinnamon, not wanting to be thought of as useless, said, "I can help too! I'm small and fast! I can bite them on their tails for you!"

Ding smiled, and Sassy laughed out loud. "I will share my dinner with you, sis, if you bite a coyote on the tail!"

The weather grew warmer; Ding continued his daily patrols around the farm. Wendy and the sergeant were bringing in more young goats for the farm as spring grew closer every day.

On the first warm night, Ding could hear Gus barking in the woods. Ding followed the barking until he could see Gus.

"They…they…here, they are here!" barked Gus as he ran toward Ding.

"Catch your breath and calm down so I can understand what you are saying!" Ding had an idea as to what was frightening his friend.

As Gus was trying to calm himself so he could talk to Ding, the howls of coyotes could be heard in the distance.

"I understand what you wanted to tell me now!" Ding said as he looked off in the direction of the howling.

CHAPTER 9

The Challenge

"My big brother is an alpha!" Tails was so excited for his brother Scout. "Before you know it, Bones, we will be in charge when Scout becomes the next leader of the pack!"

"*Shut up!*" Scout yelled at his brothers, and they came into sight of the farm. "The first thing I'm going to do is put that horse in her place! I am an alpha now, and she will show me respect!" Scout turned to look at his brothers with a sinister grin. "Then I'll take Snow as my bride and replace that father of hers as the chief!"

"Yeah! Then we will be in charge!" Bones answered with a smile.

"*No!* Just me! And only me!" Scout yelled as he hit both of his brothers in the face. "First thing I'm going to do in the morning is go see that old horse!" Bones and Tails continued to follow their brother back to their den to rest for the night.

Up ahead of the pack leading the way to the summer hunting grounds was the chief and Snow. The chief knew it was time for his daughter to pick a mate this summer, and he really wished her mother was still here to help him with this discussion. He knew that she would resist the idea of being forced into marriage. "Snow, it's time for you to pick a mate, one who can rule by your side and become the next chief."

Shocked that he would bring it up now, she stepped out in front of her father to face him. "Marriage! Never! None of these alphas are even good enough to beat me in a fight!"

The chief knew what her answer would be. "You are as stubborn as your mother!" he said with a smile.

"I know you never challenged my mother on anything!" Snow said, still upset with the demands of her father. "She even told me that the one fight you did have before you got married, you lost!"

Laughing out loud, the chief replied, "You are right! I did lose the fight with her! But that's not how I won her hand in marriage! I won it because I was the only one who completed the challenge she put out in front of the alpha suitors."

Snow had never heard how her parents had become married and was eager to hear the story. "She never told me about a challenge?"

The chief smiled at his daughter. "Come, walk with me, and I will tell you the story of your mother."

As they continued the journey home, Snow walked alongside her father as he told her the story.

"Your mother and Jesse were very good friends. So together, they came up with the idea of how she would decide who to marry. Jesse had your mother go and pick out a flower that she liked. When she returned, Jesse told that the one she married would not only have to be the bravest of the alphas but also the smartest. Jesse advised her that she would put the flower in her stall, and the alpha suitors would have to retrieve it and bring it to her. So that night at the council meeting in front of my father and the rest of the alphas, she told us what we would have to do to win her hand in marriage. The chief agreed to the challenge and gave the alpha suitors seven days to retrieve the flower from Jesse's stall. One by one, I watched each suitor try and sneak in to retrieve the flower from the barn. But they all failed.

"That horse left hoofprints on everyone who dared to enter her barn. I knew that I would not stand a chance either to try and sneak by that horse. So as I watched Jesse every day, trying to figure out how to retrieve the flower, I noticed that Jesse had a weakness. There's an apple tree just outside the barn, and that old horse loved apples. She would go up to that tree every day and try to get an apple. But they were always just out of her reach.

"I knew I could not climb up that tree and get her the apples she wanted, but I knew someone who could. So I made a deal with Jesse. If I could get her all the ripe, juicy apples from the tree, she would trade me the apples for the flower. She agreed, so I told her I would be back tomorrow night and retrieve the apples for her.

"There was no time to waste because I was going to need help with getting those apples, and I needed someone who could climb a tree. I knew of a family of raccoons that lived down by the river. I ran down to the river as quickly as I could for there was only one night left to win the challenge.

"When I arrived at the river, I found the father of the raccoon family trying to catch a fish for his family. I told him, 'The fish you are trying to catch are too small to feed your family. If I were to catch you one big fish, it would feed your entire family. I only ask that you do something for me in return.' He asked me why a coyote would need help from a raccoon. So I told him of the challenge and how I needed his help to win your mother's hand in marriage. He agreed to help me if I could bring him two big fish. So off I went to try and get two fish. What I didn't know was that catching the fish would not be as easy as I thought, but I was determined to catch them. It took me all night and most of the next day to catch those fish. I was so wet from doing it I didn't think my fur would ever dry. I returned with the two fish, and the raccoon's family was very happy to see that the fish were longer than me. He said, 'These fish will feed my family for two weeks, thank you very much.'

"With the day already half gone, the raccoon and I left for the farm. The sun had just set when we arrived. I told Jesse how the raccoon agreed to help her retrieve the apples from the tree, and she also got a good laugh when I told her what I had to do to have the raccoon help get her the apples. So Jesse lowered her head over the fence and picked up the raccoon and took him to the tree. The raccoon climbed up the tree and picked all the ripe apples for her, and in return, she not only gave me the flower but she also let the raccoon take some of the apples home to his family.

"The flower Jesse was safeguarding was a white rose. That rose was as white as you and as beautiful as your mother. I thanked Jesse and the raccoon and ran as fast as I could back home.

"I arrived just in time for the council meeting. I entered the meeting and laid the rose down in front of your mother and asked her, 'If this is your flower, then will you accept it as my proposal to be my bride!' She smiled and said yes. The next night under the full moon, we exchanged vows and became husband and wife."

Snow stopped to look at the moon. "I do miss her!" She said as a tear came from her eye.

The chief stopped to comfort his daughter. "I miss her too, and you have a lot of her in you!" Smiling at Snow, he said, "You have your mother's beauty, you are just as stubborn as her, but most of all, you are just as smart as she was. And I know that in your own way, you will make the right decision for a mate."

Leaning on her father, Snow said, "Thank you, Father! I promise to let you know what I decided to do!"

CHAPTER 10

The Family Grows

Ding was up with the sun, but this time, he started his patrol with a stop by the barn. He entered through the top and went down the stairs to the stalls where the goats were still asleep. From the steps, he could count the goats.

"I see you are still getting up with the sun," the sergeant was coming downstairs to do the morning chores.

Charles went to the back of the stall. "Ding! Was that you howling last night?"

Ding came down to the bottom step. "No, what you heard last night were the howls of coyotes!"

Charles, remembering what his mother had told him about coyotes, got nervous. "My mother told me about them. You don't think they can get in here, do you?"

"No, they cannot get to you!" Ding replied, trying to calm down the young goat. "Besides, they have to get past the sergeant and me first!"

"Yes, they do!" Sassy said as she and Cinnamon came down the steps. "We are all working together!"

"Come on, you three, it's time to get to work!" the sergeant said as he opened the barn door. "Now go chase the goats out of the stalls so I can clean."

Cinnamon loved chasing the goats out of the barn. "*Bark! Bark!* I love chasing goats! *Bark! Bark!*"

Once everyone was out, Cinnamon would stand guard at the door to make sure the goats didn't go back in until the sergeant was done. Ding and Sassy would watch over the goats and enjoy the morning sun.

Charles, being followed by Jane, wanted to talk more about what to do if they saw the coyotes. "What should we do if we see any coyotes?"

Sassy stood up, looking at both goats. "Both Jane and you are the alphas of the group. The other goats will be looking to you as to what they should do. Jane, it will be up to you to get the does to safety in the barn, and Charles, you have those horns on your head for a reason, so if they get too close, drop your head and hit them!"

Jane knew the other does all looked up to her. "Thank you, Sassy. If we see anything, we will make a lot of noise to get Ding's and your attention!"

Ding and Sassy turned around to answer the call from the sergeant. "Come on, guys, we are done!"

As they exited the barn, Sassy spotted some old friends flying toward the pond and took off running with Cinnamon right behind her. Ding followed the sergeant down to the machine shed. It was time to get the fields ready to plant the corn.

As the sergeant entered the machine shed, Ding was struck in the head by a walnut.

"Hey! You dog!" yelled Jack from a tree next to the shed.

Looking up and rubbing his head, Ding said, "I have a name, and it's Ding! If you want my attention, just say my name and don't throw a walnut!"

"Sorry! I really am!" Jack came down out of the tree. "I know our friend is gone, and the family wants to offer our help. We can keep watch for you from the trees and let you know if we see anything suspicious!"

Ding lowered his head down to the little chipmunk. "I would appreciate the help so long as you don't throw any more nuts at me!"

"Promise! No more nuts!" Jack quickly ran back up the tree just as the sergeant was coming out of the shed with the tractor.

The sergeant got out of the tractor and lifted Ding up into the cab, and off they went to prepare the ground for planting.

Sassy looked at Cinnamon as they approached the pond. "Okay, we are going to lie down here in the high grass and wait for them!"

The ducks circled the pond in preparation for their landing. "We are finally here, Fran. I can't wait to rest my wings!"

"Oh no, you don't!" Fran said, looking at her husband. "You are going to help me get the nest ready before you take a nap!"

"Fine!" Sam replied as they landed in the water.

"So when are we going to jump out and scare the ducks?" The overzealous Cinnamon was not very patient at waiting.

"We are not going to scare them!" Sassy whispered to Cinnamon. "We are going to ask for their help with the coyotes!"

"Help?" Cinnamon didn't understand.

"Trust me!" Sassy whispered, smiling. "Okay! We will scare them one more time!"

"Who are we going to scare!"

Both Sassy and Cinnamon jumped into the air, screaming in fright. As they turned around, they saw their friend Gus lying down, laughing. Even Sam and Fran were laughing as they swam over to Sassy and Cinnamon.

"Gus!" Sassy said, giggling. "We never heard you come up behind us!"

Gus, still laughing, said, "I know!"

"We were going to surprise the ducks!" muttered Cinnamon.

"Now that you have given us a good laugh," Sam's voice is getting more serious, "why are you here?"

Sassy walked up to the edge of the water. "I came to apologize for biting your tail and to let you know that our friend Jesse passed away this winter."

Fran, gasping, leaned her head against her husband and began to cry. Sam, holding his wife, tried to give her comfort. "I accept your apology and thank you for letting us know about Jesse."

With a look of seriousness, Sassy asked, "There is one more thing I would like to ask of you. With your ability to fly, can you please let us know if you see any coyotes near the farm?"

Fran raised her head and drifted over to Sassy as she dried her tears. "Yes, for you, for the farm, and in honor of our friend Jesse, we will help!"

"Thank you! Now what are you doing here, Gus?" Sassy asked as she turned around.

"For the stories!" Gus happily answered, wagging his tail.

"Sam and Fran, tell…tell me about there adven…adven… adventure when they return every year!"

"Stories! I love stories! Can I hear them too!" Cinnamon asked as she jumped to her feet and started wagging her tail with excitement.

"Why, of course, you can stay and listen!" Fran answered. "We will tell you as we repair our nest!"

Gus and Cinnamon followed the ducks around the pond while Sassy left to go to the machine shed to wait for Ding.

The sound of the farm tractor coming in from the field woke Sassy up. The sergeant stepped out of the cab and lowered Ding down to the ground. While the sergeant pulled the tractor into the shed, Ding and Sassy talked about how their day had been.

CHAPTER 11

Respect

As the sun set, Scout had sent his brothers off to find Gus. A while later, with Tails leading the way and his brother Bones carrying poor Gus in his mouth, they met back up with Scout.

As they approached Scout, Tails was prancing around, singing, "We did what our brother asked, and we caught the stuttering fox! We did what our brother asked, and we caught the stuttering fox!"

"Will you shut up!" Scout growled at Tails. "Toss him over here!" Bones threw Gus down at Scout's feet. "I need you to go and tell that dumb horse that Scout the Alpha is here!"

Gus jumped to his feet as quickly as he could and took off running. Gus went up to the edge of the woods and could see Ding walking back toward the farmhouse. Gus howled to get Ding's attention.

Walking over to the edge of the woods, Ding could see that Gus was scared. "They…they…they are here to see Jesse!"

"Okay! Gus, let's calm down first. Take a deep breath and let it out!" Now that Ding had him a little bit calmer, he asked, "Now tell me who's here?"

"They call him Scout! He is the biggest of the three brothers and the meanest of all the coyotes!" Gus was still shaken up from the way the coyotes treated him. "He…he…he wants to see Jesse! He's waiting for her in the…the corner of the backwoods!"

"Why don't you stay here tonight? You can sleep in the upper part of the barn!" Ding said, pointing to the old red barn. "I'm going to go have a look at these coyotes!" Gus nodded his head and headed for the barn while Ding crept quietly into the woods.

"Where is that stubborn horse!" Scout's anger and voice grew the more he had to wait. Scout began pacing back and forth along the fence. He grabbed Bones by his tail and threw him into the air. Tails knew when his brother was this angry that the only safe place was back home. Tails helped Bones get up, and together, they ran home. "Get back here you cowards!" Scout shouted at them as he grabbed a small branch and flung it over the fence.

"He really has a temper, doesn't he, Ding?" Jack said, whispering to Ding.

Ding replied, looking at Jack who was standing next to where he was hiding in the tall grass, "Yes, he does. And when did you get here?"

"I left when you did!" Jack replied as he climbed on top of Ding's head. "I may be old, but I can move through the trees just as fast as you can run!"

Just then, Scout tossed another small branch over the fence and nearly hit them. "Jesse! I am an *alpha*! *I will not be ignored by you! Show yourself now!*" Off in the distance, a single howl could be heard. Scout stomped his front paws on the ground. "*I will be back! And you will give me the respect I deserve!*"

As Scout disappeared into the night, they could still hear him throwing stuff. Ding stood up from his hiding spot. "Where is he going?"

Jack turned Ding's left ear. "The coyotes are being called home. They have to go when the leader of the pack calls!"

"Well, then, maybe we should go home too?" Ding turned around to head home. "Would you like a ride?"

Jack stretched out and got comfortable between Ding's ears. "Sure!"

On the walk back home, Jack told Ding everything he knew about the coyotes and the one they called Scout.

Once inside, Ding found Sassy and Cinnamon in the family room, watching television with the family. "Gus showed up tonight and said that there was a coyote here looking for Jesse. They scared him pretty good."

"Is he all right!" Cinnamon asked.

As Ding lay down next to Sassy, he replied, "Yes, he's asleep out in the barn. He knows to get out before the family goes out there to do the morning chores."

"So did you see the coyotes, and do they know about Jesse?" Sassy asked, wanting to know more about what had transpired tonight.

"No, they don't know!" Ding answered. "And that seems to have made this coyote they call Scout very angry! Angry enough that he threw one of his brothers into the air, and the other one took off running into the night. After his brothers left him, he continued to grow madder by the minute because Jesse was not coming out to see him. He kept yelling for Jesse to show herself and give him respect!"

"Respect is not given. It's something you earn from those around you!" Cinnamon answered with a look of pride on her face.

Sassy turned to Cinnamon in shock. "That's the first smart thing I have ever heard you say! Now go to sleep and rest that brain cell!"

Cinnamon sat up. "Why, thank you! I think?"

Looking back over to Ding, Sassy still wanted to hear more about the coyotes. "So what did this Scout look like?"

"You are too old for a boyfriend!" Cinnamon said.

Growling at Cinnamon, Sassy said while trying to show her good side, "That's not why I'm asking. But you never know!"

Giving them both a stern look, Ding said, "If you two are done? I couldn't see the other two very well, but Scout was my height and size, and his fur was as black as the night. Jack said the other two brothers of his are Tails and Bones. Tails is smaller than Gus and has a tail long enough to wrap himself in it. Bones is shorter than Scout, is very thin, and tends not to talk much. They follow their big brother everywhere and will do anything he asks. So long as they believe that Jesse is still alive, they will not come through the fence. Jack said that they are afraid of the fence too."

"Afraid of the fence?" Sassy asked. "Why are they afraid of a fence?"

"Jack said that there was a time when the fence would shock you. But the old farmer turned it off a long time ago!" Ding answered.

"Come on, Sassy, it's time for bed!" Anna called for her as she and Chey headed upstairs.

As Sassy followed the girls, Cinnamon left with Wendy and the sergeant, and Ding made himself comfortable on the couch. He was ready for a good night's sleep.

CHAPTER 12

The Moon

"Auntie Snow! Auntie Snow!" all the puppies were calling her name, and as she lay down, they gathered around her.

"We want to hear a story!" one of the puppies said.

"Okay! And what would you like to hear about?" she asked.

One little puppy who was still sitting up asked, "Why do we howl at the moon?"

"So you want to know? Well, gather around, and I will tell you!" she said, smiling.

"The moon is the eye of the great coyote god. When his eye is fully opened, all those who have passed away are able to look down and see the loved ones that they left behind. So when the moon is full, we howl to those friends and family members. When they hear your howl, they are able to find you. And I heard that sometimes when the moon is full, they are even able to come and visit us."

"I see you have your mother's gift of storytelling!" her uncle said as he approached her. "Your stories put them right to sleep every time."

Snow carefully stood up so as not to wake up the puppies. "So how did the council meeting go?" Snow asked as she went over and sat next to her uncle.

As he looked at her, he said, "They were asking your father if you had chosen a mate. But don't worry, he let them know that you will be married before the winter comes."

"I know I'm the chief's daughter, and so everyone is trying to get me to choose, and I will, when I find the right one!"

Snow replied, "I want the one I choose to be brave, strong, and smart. But most of all, he must have a heart that he listens to!"

Her uncle looked up at the moon. "I'm sure my sister is looking down here right now, and she will help guide you in your decision. Well, good night, Snow!"

"Good night, Uncle." Snow stayed sitting there, staring at the moon.

As she headed home, she walked by where all the young alpha males were settling in for the night. As she walked past them swinging her tail, they raised their heads to watch.

"Hello there, Snow!" Scout said as he stepped out of the shadows. "Are you ready to become my bride?"

She stopped right in front of Scout and sat down with her back to him. "What makes you think you are going to be my husband? Especially when I have so many of you to choose from!"

The other alphas began to stand up. Scout quickly stood in front of Snow and growled at the other alphas. As he stood there growling at them, they all lay down, hiding their heads under their tails. Once he had established his dominance over them, he turned back to Snow. "As you can see, there are no other alphas who are interested in you. I am the strongest and most feared of all the alphas. So it's only right that the chief's daughter be married to me."

Snow, who was now standing, said, "It takes more than fear and strength to be an *alpha*!" Now Scout was setting down as Snow circled around him. "You still don't know what it takes to be a leader of a pack! To be the leader of a pack, you have to be brave, strong, smart, and most of all, you have to have earned their respect! And to do that, you have to have a heart!" Snow stopped right in front of him as he cringed. "You have none of it! I will never marry you!" Snow flipped her tail at Scout as she walked away from him.

Scout noticed the other alphas were staring at him. "What are you looking at!" They quickly put their heads down.

Instead of going inside her den she shared with her father, Snow stayed outside, looking up at the crescent moon, hoping that her mother was listening. "Mother, I know what is expected of me and what my duties are as the daughter of the chief. But it's time like this I wish you were here."

"I saw what happened with Scout," her father said as he came out of the den and sat beside her. "You handled the situation like a true leader."

"Thank you, Father," Snow replied as she rested her head on her father. "Do you think Mom is really up there watching over us?"

Leaning his head on hers, her father said, "Yes! She is always watching!"

CHAPTER 13

Family

Sassy found Ding behind the machine shed, sitting on a tree that had fallen down years ago. "Can you see him?"

"No." Ding put his nose into the wind. "But I can smell him! Every day when Sam takes his afternoon flight, he sees him and his brothers just sitting on top of a hill out there, just looking down at the farm. What is he waiting for?"

Up on top of a hill, Scout had been sitting, watching the farm. While he sat there, staring down at the farm, his two brothers would be back behind him, playing like two young pups. "It's time!" he said, turning around to his brothers. "The corn is finally high enough to give us cover. This evening, we will go down by the barn fence and see why Jesse ignored me!"

Tails stopped playing and ran up to his brother Scout. "But that's dangerous! What if the farmer sees us?"

Scout turned his head slightly to his brother. "I'm not scared of the farmer or his iron stick!"

As Scout headed down the hill, Tails and Bones looked at each other. Without saying a word, they knew the dangers of being seen by the farmer. "Come on, Tails, we can't let him go alone!" Bones said as he walked past Tails.

"I don't smell him anymore. He's on the move!" Ding looked over to Sassy. "Go ask Sam if he would fly out there and see if he can find Scout and his brothers. I'm going to go out into the woods and look around!"

Off Sassy went to the pond while Ding made a patrol of the woods. "Good I found you!" Sassy was a little tuckered out from the running.

Sam was enjoying a nap on the pond when she arrived. "Well, I'm glad to see you too."

Sassy was still a little winded. "I'm getting too old to run like this anymore! Ding would like to know if you would fly out and see if you can find Scout and his brothers. He said they have moved off the hill."

Stretching his wings, Sam agreed to see if he could locate the coyotes for Ding. Off Sam took into the air, in search of the coyotes. Sassy went over to where Fran was nesting to wait for his return.

As the sunlight faded, Sam returned. Swimming over to Fran and Sassy, he said, "I saw other coyotes, but I never found Scout and his brothers."

Sassy stood up and walked over to the edge of the water. "Thank you for looking, I will let Ding know."

While Sassy waited for Ding by the farmhouse, Wendy, the girls, and Cinnamon came out to go feed the goats. "Come on, Sassy, you can help!" Anna said.

Just on the other side of the fence, lying hidden in the tall grass, were Scout and his brothers.

"Scout, I don't see Jesse! Just a bunch of goats!" Tails mouth was beginning to water over the thought of eating goats.

Scout looked over at Tails. "I need you to stand right in front of me!"

Tails stood up and with his back to Scout. "Okay! Now what do you want me to do?" Just then, Scout shoved Tails into the fence. Tails bounced off the fence and right back into Scout.

"What did you do that for!"

Scout quickly grabbed Tails and covered his mouth. "Be quiet!" he whispered in Tails's ear. "The fence is not working. We can get in!"

All the goats heard the noise, including Sassy and Cinnamon. Charles went over to investigate, along with Sassy and Cinnamon.

Standing near where they had heard the noise, Sassy and Cinnamon sniffed around while Charles watched. Neither Sassy nor Cinnamon could smell anything, so the three of them thought maybe a walnut had fallen and hit the fence.

"We are downwind. They can't smell us!" Scout said, smiling. "And now I know why Jesse never came!" As he looked at both his brothers, he said, "It's obvious. She didn't survive the winter."

"Cinnamon! Sassy! Come here!" Wendy needed their help to get the goats away from the feed pans so she could feed them.

Scout saw this as an opportunity. He quickly began digging while everyone was distracted. Motioning for his brothers, they crawled underneath the fence.

Chey came out of the barn and began filling the goats' water tank. As she looked around, she saw the coyotes crawling under the fence. *"Mom! Mom! Coyotes!"*

Wendy ran out of the barn with a pitchfork in her hands. "Chey! Anna! Go up through the barn and get to the house! Anna, I need you to bring me the gun!"

Jack was in a nearby tree and climbed out onto the edge of the branch; he was on to see what all the commotion was about. As soon as he saw the coyotes, he yelled out to his family to alert Ding to the danger. As Anna and Chey made their way to the house, they could hear the trees above them come to life with the chatter of the chipmunks. Ding also could hear it, as the noise came toward him like a wave splashing against the beach. Ding went over to a nearby tree where he saw a chipmunk coming down the trunk. "Coyotes are after the goats!" Ding immediately took off running for the corral.

The sergeant was coming up the driveway and saw Ding running toward the corral in his headlights. Thinking nothing of it, he parked his truck and went into the house where he was greeted by the girls. After they told him what was happening, he grabbed his gun from the cabinet and ran to the corral with both girls following him.

Ding could see Wendy, Sassy, and Cinnamon trying to stop Tails and Bones from getting inside the barn where the does were seeking shelter from the coyotes and that Charles was lying on the ground, bleeding from trying to fend off Scout. After jumping over the gate into the corral, Ding raced toward Scout. Ding caught Scout in midair just as he was jumping onto Charles's back. Scout went tumbling to the ground.

Ding, looking down at Charles, said, "It's okay now. I'm here!"

Lying there on the ground, Scout could feel the blood trickling down from his ear where Ding had torn it open. Picking himself up off the ground, he looked over at Ding. "You tore my ear, farm dog!"

The two dogs began to circle each other, looking for a weakness in the other.

"I've never seen a farm dog like you before?" Scout was curious about what Ding's breed was. "Just what breed of farm dog are you?"

"I'm a dingo, and my name is Ding! Not farm dog!" Ding growled.

"Never heard of your breed. But it's not going to matter, farm dog. You will be dead soon enough!" Scout said with an evil grin, just before he attacked him.

Ding stepped to the side and grabbed Scout by his tail as he went by. With Scout's tail in his mouth, he swung Scout into the air and back onto the ground again. Scout was becoming frustrated that a farm dog was getting the best of him. As he began to stand up, a shot rang out, and dirt flew into his face as the bullet struck the ground in front of him.

Hearing the gunshot scared Tails and Bones. They exchanged a glance as they both knew it was time to leave. As they ran past Scout, they yelled for him to follow them.

"Your brothers know when it's time to leave!" Ding growled, "The next one may not be a warning!"

"Don't kill him, please!" Chey asked the sergeant as he raised his gun again.

He lowered his gun, looking down at Chey; as he wiped a tear from her cheek, he could see the concern in her eyes. "I promise I will not kill the coyote, but I must scare him off!" As he raised his gun, he told the girls to cover their ears.

"I'm not scared of a farmer with an iron stick!" growled Scout.

Scout and Ding now engaged in a fierce battle. As the battle continued on, Ding bit down on Scout's neck and flung him to the ground. Scout wasted no time to get back on his feet, and as he jumped at Ding, the sergeant fired his gun. And Scout fell to the ground.

Scout, lying on the ground, could feel the pain; as he looked back behind him, rising to his feet, he could see his tail lying on the ground. Scout, looking around, knew he had lost the battle for now. "This is not over, farm dog! I will be back!" Scout turned and left back the way he had come in.

Ding picked up the tail and tossed it over the fence. When he turned back around, he could see everyone was okay. Wendy and the sergeant were tending to Charles' scratch marks; the other does were coming out of the barn, running over to Charles, calling him their hero. Sassy and Cinnamon were being loved on by Anna and Chey; even the chipmunks were cheering from the trees.

"I finally understand! I see what Sassy was telling me! I was never alone. I have family and friends who are always here to help!"

The sergeant motioned to everyone. "Come on, everyone, I think that's enough excitement for one night!"

CHAPTER 14

Disgrace

Scout never said a word as he led his brothers back home. As Scout walked past the other young alpha males, he could feel their stares as he walked by. All of a sudden, they started laughing.

"What are you all laughing at!"

Here came Tails, walking toward him, carrying his tail.

Snarling at Tails, Scout said, "Why do you have that? Get rid of it!"

Tails dropped the bloody tail onto the ground, only to have the other alphas pick it up. Tails tried to get it back, but the other alphas were so much taller than him.

The laughter drew the attention of the council and Snow. With the chief leading the way, they saw Tails and Scout trying to retrieve the tail.

"Whose tail is that?"

Everyone froze when they heard the chief's voice. Snow, not wanting to be seen, hid behind a bush. She could see that Scout had been in a fight, and not only was he missing a tail but she could see that one of his ears had been split in two as well.

Snow's uncle stepped forward, looking at the young alphas. "Well, answer your chief!"

All the young alphas turned and looked at Scout.

As Scout walked through the alphas, Tails grabbed the tail and followed his brother and placed the tail at his brother's feet. "It is mine!"

The chief walked over to Scout, looking at his bloody face and the tail that was lying at his feet. "What pack of coyotes did this to you?"

Scout, lowering his head, thinking about how a farm dog had defeated him, said, "It was not another coyote. It was a farmer who shot off my tail and his dog who tore my ear in half!" Now feeling the anger building inside of him, he said, "And as soon as I heal, I will have my revenge against that dingo!"

"Did you say dingo? Was the breed of this dog a dingo?" The chief anxiously waited for an answer.

"Yes! My opponent said he was a dingo. But there is no such breed, is there?" Scout raised his head as to why there was so much concern about one farm dog.

The council quickly huddled around the chief. Everyone now was intrigued about all the discussion over one dog. Scout and the rest of the young alphas tried to lean into the huddle to hear what they were talking about.

As the council broke from its huddle, the chief stepped forward. "Yes, there was a time when the dingoes roamed these lands. They were brave, strong, and cunning hunters that traveled in packs. Then man came and was befriended by the dingoes. As man became more dominant over the land, the dingoes slowly disappeared. Tomorrow, the council and I will go and see this farm dog and determine whether or not he is a dingo. In the meantime, all coyotes are to stay away from the land the dingo lives on. Now you, Scout, will go and heal your wounds, and the rest of you, get some rest." As the council left with the chief, they continued their discussion about the return of the dingo.

Once her father and the council were gone, Snow headed home, thinking about what had happened to Scout. "What happened to Scout should not have happened to any coyote! The council and my father said that Scout and the other alpha males could not seek revenge, but he did not say that the females of the pack were not allowed!"

CHAPTER 15

Love Is in the Air

The next morning, Wendy and the sergeant were both up doing the morning chores. As the sergeant cleaned the stalls, Wendy checked on Charles's wounds from the night before. Once the chores were done, Ding headed off for his daily patrols while Sassy and Cinnamon followed Wendy and the sergeant.

When Ding reached the woods, Gus was there waiting for him. "I heard what happened last night from the chipmunks!"

"Yeah, with everyone working together, we were able to scare them off!" Ding replied.

As Ding continued his patrol, Gus tagged along with him to hear more about what had happened the night before.

Sassy and Cinnamon were relaxing by the pond, chatting with Sam and Fran, when they saw a rabbit running across the yard, heading toward the machine shed. Chasing rabbits was something that they both liked to do together. They knew that they were never going to catch it; all the fun was in the chase. Off they went after the little cottontail.

"Don't follow the rabbit out into the cornfield, you can get lost in it!" Sam yelled as they took off.

"You better keep an eye on them two!" Fran was concerned that they would not stop at the back gate and continue to follow the rabbit out into the corn.

Sam took off into the air to watch his friends and to look around for any coyotes.

After a while, Sam could see Cinnamon and Sassy had given up on the chase and were enjoying a nap under the afternoon sun. As he continued his air patrols, he could see something moving through the cornfield. Sam flew in low, just above the top of the corn. On his third pass over the corn, a coyote jumped up in front of him. Sam just barely evaded the coyote. Sam immediately flew back to where he had last seen Sassy and Cinnamon to warn them that a coyote was nearby, but they had already left. Sam checked the farm and even flew by Fran to see if she had seen them come home. But she had not. Sam began to fly low in the woods, looking for Ding.

"Look! Here comes Sam!" Gus pointed at Sam as he approached.

Sam landed in front of Ding and Gus and quickly told them about the coyote and how he feared that Sassy and Cinnamon might be lost in the cornfield with a coyote nearby.

Ding and Gus both ran toward the machine shed and squeezed out through the field gate in search of their friends. As they reached the cornfield, they split up in search of Sassy and Cinnamon.

"I thought you knew the way home?" Cinnamon asked.

"I thought I did!" Sassy said, sitting down, scratching her head. "Let's go this way!"

With Sassy leading the way and Cinnamon following close behind her, they came out of the corn and back into the waterway.

"I think we are back where we started from?" Sassy said as she looked around.

Cinnamon crawled out of the corn, tired from being lost. "I'm tired. Let's just call for Ding!"

So together, they howled for help, hoping Ding would hear them. Ding and Gus, both hearing the howls of Cinnamon and Sassy, began heading toward them.

"Thanks for helping me find you!"

Sassy and Cinnamon turned around. Just a few feet away, coming toward them, was an all-white coyote.

"My name is Snow, and I am here to get revenge for what one of you did to my friend Scout!" Snow told them as she crept closer to them.

Cinnamon ran behind Sassy as she stepped forward to take on the coyote. "He deserved what happened to him!"

As Sassy and Snow got closer to each other, all of a sudden, coming out of the corn, came Ding. He dropped his head and hit Snow in the side, sending her tumbling to the ground.

"I see you two are making new friends without me!" Ding said as he walked over to Cinnamon and Sassy.

Getting back on her feet, Snow looked over and could see the dingo she was looking for. "Don't you think that was a little rude to blindside me like that?"

Ding, turning back around, said, "Don't you think you should—"

"You should what?" Snow asked as she prepared to fight. "What is wrong with him?"

Sassy walked around to the front of Ding. He was just standing there with his tail wagging and his mouth wide open with his tongue hanging out. "Hey! Lover boy! Ding, snap out of it!" Sassy said as she smacked his face.

Cinnamon, poking her head out around Ding, said, "What's wrong with Ding?"

"He's in love!" Sassy answered.

"*Love!* With her! But she wants to eat us!" the nervous Cinnamon answered.

Looking back at Cinnamon, Sassy said, "No! She's not going to eat us!" Sassy went over to where Snow was standing. "Can you give us just a minute or so to bring Ding back down to earth?"

Snow stood there, not understanding what was happening. "I guess! But what is wrong with your friend!"

With a polite smile, Sassy answered, "Oh! You know! Young boy sees a pretty girl and falls in love! And by the way, you are not going to eat us, are you?"

"Why, no! I'm just here to fight! And who's he in love with?" Snow thought she knew the answer already.

"By the way, you are blushing, I think, you know?" Sassy answered as she went back over to Ding.

"Cinnamon! Bite him on the tail!" Sassy told her.

With a big smile on her face, she jumped up and bit Ding on the tail as hard as she could. Cinnamon went flying into the cornfield as Ding jumped and screamed in pain. "Well, glad you are back, lover boy! Now do you see that pretty white coyote over there?" Sassy asked, slapping his face again. "She's here to get revenge for what you did to her boyfriend, Scout!"

"Oh! She is!" Ding said, moving Sassy to the side.

"Okay! You go fight the girlfriend, and I will go check on Cinnamon!" Sassy said as she headed off to find her sister.

Ding lowered his head as he approached her, ready for battle. "So you're Scout's girlfriend! Do you have a name besides Scout's girlfriend?"

"Girlfriend! He wishes!" she answered as Ding approached. "I'm nobody's girlfriend! There is not a male around here I can't beat in a fight! And my name is Snow!"

"Glad to meet you Snow, mine is Ding!" he said, standing in front of her. "I'm sorry you had to wait so long to lose!"

Snow started walking around Ding, laughing. "You think you can defeat me. All you boys are the same. You think us girls need a big strong boy to protect us!"

Ding sat down and turned his back to Snow. "I will make this a fair fight for you. I will sit here with my back to you and my eyes closed."

"Now that's not a fair fight, but if you insist on being a foolish dingo, I won't stop you!" Snow said, smiling.

"I'm trying to be kind to Scout's girlfriend!" Ding replied.

That angered Snow. "I'm not his *girlfriend*!" she yelled as she leaped toward Ding.

Ding, listening closely, ducked and stepped backward. As Snow flew over his head, Ding stood up on his back legs, and with his front paws, he pushed against Snow's stomach, causing her to land on her back.

"Brother, she apparently is not a match for the dingo!" Snow's uncle said.

The chief nodded. "Yes, she is not, but it is time she learns defeat and some humiliation. The dingo is not going to hurt her. Look at them. He has been smiling and wagging his tail ever since he laid eyes on her. And now Snow is smiling and wagging her tail!"

Sassy found Cinnamon lying next to Gus. "What are you two doing?"

Gus raised his head to answer as Cinnamon continued to snuggle up against him. "She's hurting!"

Sassy, shaking her head, said, "No, she's not! Now let's go! Ding needs us!"

CHAPTER 16

Father

Even though Snow was becoming frustrated and tired from being tossed to the ground, she was having fun. She had finally met her match, but she was not about to give up. The more Ding would ask if she was ready to submit to defeat, the harder she would attack.

"That's Snow!" Gus told Sassy and Cinnamon as they came out of the cornfield. "She is the da-da-daughter of the le-le-leader of the pack!" Gus said, pointing to the coyotes coming out of the cornfield. "And he's here!"

"Enough!" the chief yelled as they all emerged from the cornfield.

"Father!" Snow yelped.

"You have been beaten by your opponent," the chief said with a stern voice as he approached her. "While you stand there battered and out of breath, your opponent hasn't even broken a sweat. It is time you accept defeat and go home."

"Yes, Father!" Snow replied. She walked over to Ding with a smile. "You beat me this time, but I will win the next one!"

"I can't wait!" Ding replied, smiling as she walked away.

The chief turned to Gus. "I have not seen you for a while. Who are your new friends?"

Gus stepped out in front of Sassy and Cinnamon. "This is Sassy, Cinnamon, and the one your daughter fought is Ding!"

"I know these two ladies have been lost for a while and could probably use a drink of water. Would you be kind enough and take them home, please, so we may talk to Ding?" the chief asked.

"I was beginning to think that the five of you were never going to come out of the cornfield!" Ding said, sitting there, smiling at the chief.

The chief walked over to Ding, giggling. "I'm guessing your keen sense of hearing gave us away? So then it's true that you are a dingo?"

Ding nodded his head. "Yes, I am! But seeing how you never came out to help your daughter and you have not said you are here for revenge, why are you here?"

"That's a very good question?" the chief said as he walked over and sat down in front of Ding. "I came to see for myself if it was true or not that the dingo was no longer extinct and to ask why the farmer and you attacked one of my pack members?"

"Attack! Scout and his brothers were the ones who attacked!" Ding replied defensively. "Scout and his brothers not only attacked the goats but they also attacked Sassy, Cinnamon, and the farmer's wife!"

"Hmmm! It seems that part of the story was not shared with us," the chief answered as he looked over at the council. "All coyotes know that we do not hunt a farmer's livestock, and we definitely do not attack a human. Disobeying those two rules would cause the farmers to see the coyotes as a threat. If we are seen as a threat, then they will start hunting us with their iron sticks. I want Jesse and you to know that what happened will not ever happen again so long as I am the leader of the pack and ask that you both accept my apology."

Ding lowered his head to wipe away a tear. "I accept your apology, but you should know that Jesse passed away during the winter."

The chief moved alongside of Ding and placed his paw on his back. "I know I speak for my entire pack. We will miss her dearly. She was a good friend to all of us coyotes. I know she would chase us off her land and even tossed a lot of us over the fence. It was kind of a rite of passage for the young coyotes to try and not get caught by her. But we always got caught by her." The chief and council began laughing, remembering how they all were caught by Jesse. "How is it that you came to live on this farm?"

"I got lost as a pup from my mother one day during a storm and found the family I now live with," Ding proudly answered.

"So you lived in a pack?" The chief was curious to know more.

"Yes!" Ding answered as he began to tell the story of how he met the sergeant and then, later in life, would be reunited with his family.

After the story, Ding showed them Jesse's grave before they parted ways for the evening. And when he got home, Sassy and Cinnamon were waiting for him. He told them what had happened, but what he failed to tell them was that he was hoping that Snow would be back tomorrow.

CHAPTER 17

The Punishment

Still sore and in pain from his battle the day before, Scout was sleeping when his brothers came and woke him up for the meeting. Limping behind his brothers, he followed them to the meeting. The chief was addressing the entire pack.

"The council and I have met with the farm dog that we were all led to believe was a dingo. After speaking with the farm dog, it was determined that he is a dingo, and his name is Ding. The dingoes are not extinct as our forefathers had led us to believe but are actually living in packs once again far from here. Ding, who had gotten separated from his pack, was found and raised by his new family. Ding and his friends now watch over the land that was once cared for by our friend Jesse. This last winter, she passed away, and we shall all miss her dearly. So I ask you to remember her tonight in your howls to the moon."

As the chief walked away with his daughter, Snow's uncle stepped forward to address the pack.

"It has been brought to the council's attention that a member of this pack was hunting goats and attacked a human. As a reminder to you all! We do not hunt a farmer's livestock, nor do we attack humans. We follow this simple law to prevent the humans from hunting us. Scout, Tails, and Bones, step forward before the council to face your punishment."

The three brothers moved forward as the rest of the pack turned their backs to them. Tails and Bones, both afraid of what the council would do, held their heads down in shame while their brother Scout held his head up high, proud of what he had done.

Only Snow's uncle, looking upon the three brothers, spoke. "You three will only be allowed to eat after everyone else has eaten. Scraps of food shall be your only meal until we arrive at the winter hunting grounds. You shall not travel beyond your home except to eat the scraps of food left behind by the others."

After the punishment was handed down, the council also turned their backs to the three brothers.

Once the three brothers were back home, Scout yelled out in anger, "That Dingo will pay with his life for the disgrace he has brought upon me!"

*****

"Snow, are you in here?"

"Auntie May!" Snow screamed as she ran out of the den to hug her.

"So tell me about him?" Auntie May asked with excitement.

"About who?" Snow replied.

"Come on, you can tell me. I can see your eyes sparkling just thinking about him!" her aunt said, nudging her.

"Oh! You mean Ding!" Snow said, blushing. "He's brave, strong, and smart!"

"And defeated you in battle!" her auntie May said, poking her in the ribs. "Look at you, my dear!" she said, grabbing her face. "You are in love. We have to get you cleaned up and smelling pretty to see him tomorrow!"

Snow put her paws on her head as she buried her face into the ground, crying. "I can't! I can't go see him! I disobeyed my father! I am grounded for a week!"

Patting her niece on the head, Auntie May said, "Nonsense! I'll deal with your father and your uncle! Now let's get you ready for your Ding! That is what you call him, ain't it?"

As she stood back up, drying her eyes, she said, "Yes! He has such a beautiful name!"

CHAPTER 18

First Date

The next day after the morning chores were done, Ding headed off for the cornfield. He was so anxious to see if he could find Snow that he had forgotten all about his daily patrols.

"Hey! Lover boy!" Sassy yelled at Ding. "Just where do you think you are going?"

Ding stopped just for a moment, but he did not answer. He just took off running again toward the cornfield with the hope of finding Snow.

*****

"Snow! Come out here, dear!" Auntie May was outside the den waiting for her. As Snow came out, she could see her auntie holding a red rose. "Here, now let me put this by your ear. Ohh! You are so beautiful!"

The chief and Snow's uncle came walking toward them. Before either of the two of them could say a word, Auntie May got right up in their faces, pointing and yelling at them. "You two stop right there! She is going to see her handsome Dingo! And if you try to stop her, you will deal with me!"

"Yes, ma'am!" they both responded.

The chief walked over to Snow and gave her a kiss on her forehead. "You are as beautiful as your mother."

After searching the cornfield for hours, Ding was about to give up all hope of ever seeing her again. Then he smelled something in the air and followed the scent, hoping it would lead him to her. There, just past the rows of corn, he could see her lying down in a clearing. When he stepped out of the corn, Ding tried to pretend like he was surprised that she was back. "Oh! You're back! Are you here for a rematch or did you come to take lessons from the victor?"

"You do know that I let you win," she replied slightly, turning her head toward him. "I understand that you boys don't like to lose to a girl, especially when your friends are watching!" Snow stood up and casually walked over to Ding and gently brushed against him. "But if you insist, I guess we could!"

Stretching his body, Ding said, "No, I'm still a little worn out from fighting these last two days!"

"Well, I definitely don't want you to get hurt fighting with me," she said as she walked underneath his nose before returning to where she was lying down. "Maybe we should just lie here and enjoy the warmth of the sun?"

Ding didn't even think twice about the offer and hastily rushed to lie down in front of her. "I was hoping to see you today and spend some time getting to know you?"

Snow, batting her eyes, said, "Were you? And what would you like to know about me?"

Ding wondered if his time spent growing up in the wild was any different than hers. "Before I got separated from my pack, I knew what life was like growing up in the wild, so what is it like for you?"

Snow took a moment to think about it. "I would say that the best part is the hunting. I enjoy the chase as much as I enjoy being able to eat that day. But also I have a responsibility, with my father being the pack leader. He's always telling me that I have to be a role model. I keep telling him that it's time for a change. That the females are just as good as the males and that I don't need a male by my side to lead the pack. There's not a single male I can't defeat in battle!"

With a big smile on his face, Ding said, "That is until I came along!"

Snow looked into his eyes, with her paw on his. "You are cute when you are trying to be funny! Now tell me, what's it like to go from living in a pack to living with humans?"

"*Hot dogs!*" Ding yelled so loud he startled Snow. "They are the best part of living with humans!"

"What is a hot dog?" Snow asked.

"You have to taste it to understand!" Ding answered as he stood up. "And as far as to what it's like to live with humans, I will show you. And don't worry, they are not home right now."

Jack saw Ding coming out of the cornfield and ran down the tree to greet him. "Hello there, Ding!" he said as he came around the machine shed. "Who's with you? Wait a minute! Ain't she a coyote?" he said, pointing at Snow.

"Snow, I'd like to introduce you to Jack. And yes, she is!" Ding answered with Snow standing by his side.

"If you like, I can have the family chase her off!" Jack was not thrilled to see a coyote around.

Ding, trying not to laugh, said, "No, there's no need for that. She is here to visit."

"You imbecile! Can't you see that he's on a date!" Mary hollered at Jack from up in the tree. "Now get back up here and leave the two love birds alone!"

Jack yelled up the tree to Mary, "Who are you calling an imbecile, you old bat!" Just before Jack ran back up the tree, he stopped to ask Snow a question. "I don't suppose you could eat her if I pushed her out of the tree?"

Laughing, Snow shook her head. As she continued to follow Ding, they headed toward the house.

Ding walked through the doggy door and poked his head out. "Just step through it!"

"You live inside with the humans?" Snow had never been inside a house before, and she had no idea that dogs and humans lived together inside.

"Yes! Now follow me." Ding led her into the kitchen. He grabbed a hold of the hand towel on the fridge and pulled it open. "Here they are!" Ding said as he pulled out a package of hot dogs.

After tearing the package of hot dogs open, he laid one down in front of Snow.

After sniffing at it, she took a bite. Without saying a word after the first bite, she ate the rest of it quickly. "That was great! More please!"

After sharing a package of hot dogs with Snow, Ding showed her the rest of the house and then took her out to meet Charles and Jane. When they approached the corral, they could see Charles all alone in the corral, pacing back and forth.

"Charles! Is something wrong?" Ding asked.

Charles ran over to the fence. "Oh! Everything is wrong! All the does are giving birth in the barn, and I don't know what to do!"

"It's okay! Us females know what to do, and I'm sure everything will be okay!" Snow said, trying to calm down the soon-to-be father.

"Who are you?" Charles was so nervous he didn't even notice Snow standing beside Ding.

"This is my friend Snow. I'm showing her around the farm!" Ding replied.

Charles lowered his head. "I'm so sorry! I just don't know how to help them!"

"It's okay. They know what to do!" Snow told him with a smile as she saw one of the does coming up from the barn with two newborn goats. "See, look!"

Charles turned around. "Jane!" he said as he took off running.

Ding could hear the sound of the sergeant's truck coming down the road. "They are coming home! Come on!" The two of them ran to the back gate. "Will I see you tomorrow?"

"Maybe!" she said as she gave him a kiss on the cheek just before leaving.

CHAPTER 19

Sisters

"Here she comes! Here she comes!" one of the young females in the pack yelled. Thanks to Aunt May, all the females knew about Snow's date, and they had been waiting all day for her to come home and tell them how it went.

Aunt May was standing in front of the females, waiting to greet her niece as she approached the group of females. As Snow came closer, her aunt May could see the huge smile on her face. "I can see by the smile that all went well!"

As Snow stood in front of her aunt, she raised her head up high. "I will never kiss and tell!"

"Oh, yes, you will, little one!" Aunt May replied as all the females gathered around.

Tails had seen the commotion going on among the females and tried his best to try and hear what Snow was saying. After several attempts, he managed to squeeze in just close enough to hear Snow say she was going back to see Ding again.

As the gathering broke up, Snow could see little Tails sitting there with a look of shock on his face. As she walked past him, she turned her head to him. "Tails, come with me, please!"

Tails got up and followed her over to today's kill. She reached down and tore off a leg from the deer and handed it to Tails. "I know your brothers and you are hungry, so take this back to them."

Without saying a word, Tails grabbed the leg and ran back to his brothers. When he returned to his brothers, he tore two pieces of meat off for Bones and himself before he woke up Scout to eat. Tails placed the deer leg in front of Scout and woke him up.

"Who gave you this?" Scout asked as he stared at the leg.

"Snow gave it to us!" Tails replied between bites.

Scout took a bit and looked over at Tails. "You see!" he said as he took another bite. "I told you she likes me!"

Tails stopped eating and just stared at Scout. Tails was not sure if he should tell him about Snow and the farm dog.

"What is it?" Scout noticed that his brother had something to say. "Stop staring at me and tell me what it is!"

Tails swallowed the food in his mouth. "She may like you, but she doesn't love you!"

"And what makes you think that?" Scout said as he raised up off the ground, growling.

"Because everyone knows she's in love with the farm dog!" Bones replied, giggling.

Tails shook in fear. "She's going back tomorrow to see him again."

"And the chief is allowing her to do this!" Scout yelled as his brothers nodded. "This cannot happen! She's mine!" he yelled as he lay back down to eat. "As soon as I heal, I will deal with that farm dog!"

*****

When Ding's family pulled in, he was there to greet them. The girls jumped out of the truck and ran inside while Wendy helped the sergeant get Sassy out. Cinnamon climbed out of the truck and told Ding that they were at the veterinarian and that something was wrong with Sassy. The sergeant carried Sassy into the house where Wendy and the girls were waiting for them. He placed Sassy down on the bed the girls had made for her.

"Look, Mommy! Baby goats!" Looking out the window, Anna could see the baby goats running around in the corral, playing. "Can we go out and see them?"

"We will all go and let Sassy get some rest," Wendy said.

Once they had all left, Cinnamon and Ding went over to Sassy to see what was wrong.

Sassy could see the concern in her friends. "I'm okay. Now don't you two worry about it. I am sixteen years old, and I have had a wonderful life being a part of this family."

Ding, looking down at Sassy, said, "You still have not answered the question of what is wrong?"

"I have cancer," Sassy calmly said as she looked up at Ding and Cinnamon. "They gave Wendy some medicine for me to help with the pain it's causing. Now if you don't mind, I would like to take a nap. The medicine makes me sleepy."

Cinnamon lay down beside her. "If you leave, I won't have anyone to argue with!"

Sassy rested her head next to Cinnamon. "I will be around long enough to remind you of how much I enjoy calling you my sister." She looked back over to Ding. "Now I know you spent the day with her, so tell us how it went!"

Ding sat down as Sassy and Cinnamon snuggled up together and told them all about Snow as they lay there together, falling asleep.

CHAPTER 20

Loss of a Sister

Ding and Snow continued to see each other every day. As the days turned into weeks and the weeks turned into a month, their love for each other grew. Ding had decided it was time to talk with her father and asked Gus if he could arrange a meeting.

The chief walked out of the cornfield into an opening where Ding was waiting. "This had better be important, young pup. As the leader of the pack, I am very busy!"

If Ding wasn't nervous enough, the tone of voice from her father made it worse. "I have asked you here to get your permission to marry your daughter."

"You what!" the chief yelled and then began to growl, taking a fighting stance. As the chief walked closer to Ding, looking like he was ready to fight, all of a sudden, he sat down in front of Ding, smiling. "Yes, son, you have my blessing!" Ding breathed a sigh of relief as the chief continued to talk. "The day you two fought, I knew right then that you were going to be the one to win her heart. I would love to stay and chat, but I have places to be, and I do believe that you have someone to go meet!"

"Yes! Yes! I do!" Ding replied as he took off running.

"*Wake up!*" Scout yelled at his brothers. "It's time to pay that farm dog a visit!" The two brothers woke up and followed Scout.

As they were walking past the other young alphas, one of them jumped out in front of Scout.

"Well, fellas, look who has finally healed!" the young alpha said, laughing. "Now where would a no-tail loser like you be going?"

"Get out of my way!" Scout snarled.

The alpha just laughed at Scout. "It's kind of hard to be scared of you anymore, especially since you lost your tail, beta!"

All the alphas began to laugh together at Scout.

Scout began to walk around the young alpha. "That's right, I have no tail!" Scout laughed as he slowly walked to the backside of the young alpha. "And look, my ear was torn in two!" Scout stood behind the unaware young alpha. "But you should remember who's in *charge*!" Scout yelled as he bit down on the tail off the young alpha and tossed him on top of the other alphas. "Now! Would anyone else like to challenge me!" he said, growling. As the alphas lay there in a pile, they all shook their heads as the three brothers walked away.

Ding could see Snow setting in between the rows of corn as he hustled toward her, carrying a white rose he had picked from Wendy's flower garden. He laid the rose down in front of her.

"Oh! Ding, this was my mother's favorite flower!" The scent of the flower brought back memories of Snow's mother as she put it by her ear.

Ding cleared his voice to prepare to ask her. "Snow, would you please sit up?" He placed his paw on hers as she sat in front of him. "This is the spot where we first met each other and the place where we fought for the first time." As he spoke, Snow's eyes began to tear up. "And this is where I would love to ask you for your hand in marriage so we may fight future challenges together!"

Snow began hugging and kissing Ding. "Yes! Yes! Yes! I would love to be your bride!"

Sam and Fran were taking a swim while Sassy lay next to the pond, relaxing. "Sam! Fran!" Sassy said, sniffing the air. "There is danger coming!" She sat looking into the woods; the two ducks took flight for safety. "You should always take a bath before you come and visit a lady, especially when you come unannounced!"

"I will make sure to do that next time!" Scout replied as he and his brothers stepped out of the woods. "Should I ever come to visit a lady!"

Sam and Fran, knowing that Sassy was in danger, decided to split up to try and find Ding.

"You may not know what a lady is!" Sassy answered as she walked between Scout and his brothers, swinging her tail, trying to buy enough time for help to arrive. "But your brothers seem to know a lady when they see one!" She said, stopping right in front of Tails, tickling his chin, causing him to blush. "You are just so cute!"

"Enough!" Scout yelled as he shoved Sassy to the ground. "And you!" he said as he slapped Tails. "She's not one of us!"

Quickly getting back on her feet, Sassy slapped Scout. "You never treat your family like that! Or a lady!"

Tails had never had someone stand up for him before or even stand up against his brother for him. Tails just stood there behind Sassy, hoping that he would not hurt her.

Sassy's slap had left a scratch mark on Scout's face. "It's time for you to learn some respect!" he growled at Sassy.

"And what kind of respect would that be!" she answered as she stood between Tails and Scout. "Is it respect that your brothers give you?"

"I have their respect!" Scout growled as he stood face-to-face with Sassy.

"That's not respect! Look at them, they don't respect you. They fear you!" Sassy replied, pointing to his brothers. "To have respect from your family, you first have to have their love!"

"I've heard enough out of you!" Scout snarled as he bit down on the back of Sassy's neck, delivering a fatal blow.

"*No!*" Gus yelled as he headbutted Scout in the ribs, sending Scout to the ground.

"Don't just stand there, get him!" Scout barked at his brothers.

As Gus fled for the woods, the chipmunks began throwing walnuts at Bones and Tails so as to help Gus escape.

Lying on the ground, Sassy began to laugh. Scout, hearing the laughter, walked over to her. "I'm glad you find dying to be funny!"

"That's not why I'm laughing!" Sassy answered as she rolled to her side, gasping. "You see, I was already dying. I have a virus that only kills dogs. And now you have it too!" She smiled up at Scout.

"Don't you feel a tingling in your body? That is the cancer virus already making its way through your body!" Sassy began laughing as Scout became nervous about what he was feeling and began scratching nervously.

"*Your lying!*" Scout yelled as Sassy drew her last breath, smiling.

Ding arrived back at the farm, only to find the rest of the family in tears as they gathered around Sassy.

CHAPTER 21

Who's Hunting Who

"Father! Father!" Snow yelled as she came running up to him with tears flowing from her eyes.

"What's wrong?" he asked, trying to comfort his daughter. "Did you and Ding have a fight?"

Snow raised her head. "No, it's far worse! Scout was at the farm, and he may have killed the farmer's dog Sassy!"

"He's gone too far this time!" Turning to Snow's uncle, he said, "Find Scout and his brothers and bring them before me!"

"Yes, chief!" Snow's uncle turned to the pack and sent them all out to find Scout and his brothers.

*****

"We can stay here tonight by the river," Scout told his brothers as he looked around, scratching at his neck. "I'm sure by now that the entire pack is out looking for us!"

Bones went over and began to look at Scout's neck. "I don't see anything. Why are you scratching so much?"

"After you two left, that farm dog said that she had a disease that kills dogs!" he said as he stopped to scratch. "She lay there, laughing at me because now I was infected with it too!" The two brothers concerned for their brother didn't know what to say. Scout began scratching against a tree. "She said the disease was called cancer!"

Both Tails and Bones fell over, laughing hysterically. "I'm glad you find my death funny!" Scout said as he continued scratching.

Bones managed to mutter out between laughs, "She may be gone, but she got the final laugh. Because you can't get cancer from biting someone!"

"I knew she was lying!" Scout felt like a fool for believing Sassy. He was missing fur from all the scratching.

"You said we were only going to scare her," Tails said, looking at Scout with his sad puppy dog eyes. "Now we can never go back home!"

"Will you shut up!" Scout replied with his demanding voice. "We will go back home just as soon as I become the leader of the pack!"

Bones, wondering how Scout's going to accomplish that, tilted his head. "How are you going to do that? Snow is in love with the dingo!"

Scout looked around to make sure they were alone. "I'm going to challenge the chief!"

"We can't go home because of you, so how are you going to fight him for the leadership of the pack?" Tails asked.

As the three of them lay down facing one another, Scout began to tell them his plan. "We have to get the chief away from the pack so he's the only one I have to fight. Right now, he's surrounded by the council trying to find us. Once the pack goes back and tells them they were unable to locate us, the chief and the council will think that we have left for good and will never return. That's when we will catch the chief. He will start going out on his own again, and then I can challenge him with no interference from the pack. After I defeat him, the pack will have no choice but to follow me, and Snow will be mine!"

*****

The chief was sitting on a hill when his brother-in-law found him.

"It's been three days, and we still haven't seen Scout and his brothers," he said as he sat next to the chief who was still hoping to find Scout. "It's time to call off the search!"

"Yes, yes, you are right," the chief replied as he stood up. "But have them stay alert for any signs of them."

The chief went to his favorite place down by the river. Here, he could clear thoughts and just relax to the sound of the river. As he sat there listening to the sounds of the river, he could hear movement behind him, coming toward him.

"Where is your brother Scout?" he asked as he turned around.

"We left him behind," Bones answered. "Tails and I want to come home. We went to the farm looking for the dingo. When Scout saw her lying next to the pond, he decided to scare her instead. But she was not afraid of him."

"She stood up for me!" Tails shouted as he wiped away the tears. "She slapped Scout for hitting me!"

"I think I understand now as to what happened," the chief said as he walked over and sat in front of the two brothers. "You two can come back, but you will still have to stay close to home. And as for your brother, I will go talk to him after I take you two home."

Scout jumped out of the brush, landing on the back of the chief. He bit down as hard as he could on the chief's neck, delivering a swift and fatal blow. With the chief's lifeless body lying by his feet, Scout just stood there, smiling. "Now! Now! I shall get the respect I deserve!" Scout looked over at his brothers. "You two played your roles perfectly. Now get over here and help lift him up so I can carry him back to the pack and take my rightful place as the leader of the pack!"

The two scared younger brothers quickly helped lift the body of the chief onto Scout's back.

CHAPTER 22

A Family's Fear

"Sir! Sir!" a young coyote hollered as he ran toward the council.

"What is it that you need, young pup?" asked Snow's uncle.

"It's Scout! He's carrying the chief!" the young coyote said as he turned and pointed back behind him.

Off in the distance, they could see Scout and his brothers coming toward them. And on his back was their chief. "You! Go and find his daughter, Snow!" said her uncle to the young coyote.

The pack began to gather around Scout and his brothers as they got closer to the council. The fallen pack leader was being carried like a trophy by Scout as he walked past the other coyotes. Once he reached the council, he tossed the chief's body to the ground in front of the council.

"I bring you back the body of our pack leader and claim the title of head alpha and leader of the pack!" Scout said to the council and the pack. "I defeated him in combat, and as the rules state, I am now the head alpha!"

"And who witnessed the battle to make sure it was truly a fair fight?" Snow's uncle asked.

Scout turned to his brother's. "They are my witnesses!"

"And you expect us to believe them?" said one of the council members. "They will say anything for you!"

"Are you questioning my brother's loyalty to the pack?" Scout growled at the council. "Does anyone else want to question their loyalty or my claim as the pack leader?" the angry Scout yelled to the pack as he turned to face them.

As the council looked out into the pack to see if they would have the support to deny Scout's position of leadership, one by one, the pack lowered their heads in respect for the new head alpha.

Snow, who had been lying down next to her father, crying, stood up and walked over to Scout and slapped him. "You're no leader! If no male will challenge you, then I will!"

Scout, rubbing his chin from the slap, began to smile and slapped Snow hard enough she fell to the ground. "Females can't lead the pack, but you will help me lead the pack as my wife!"

"*Never!*" Snow yelled as she stood back up. "I will never marry you!" Snow turned around and took off running.

"You two!" Scout yelled at two young males. "Bring back my bride!" As the two young males left to retrieve Snow, he pointed to some females nearby. "You females will prepare my bride for her wedding. We will be married tonight!"

"You can't force my niece to marry you!" her uncle said. "I will not allow it, and the council will not allow it either!"

"I'm sorry, I forgot about you and the council," Scout said with a smile. "Your assistance as council members is no longer needed."

"You can't disband the council!" her uncle said.

Scout slowly walked toward the council, grinning. "No, I can't! But I can replace you!" He turned toward his brothers. "They shall be my new council!"

So Snow's uncle knew there was nothing the council could do to stop Scout. He turned to the council with an idea of how to stop Scout; he motioned for the others to follow him.

"Is there not anything we can do to stop him?" one of the council members asked.

Snow's uncle looked around to make sure they were alone. "Yes, there is someone who can challenge Scout for the leadership of the pack. And that someone is Ding!"

With a look of shock on their faces, one of them said, "A farm dog cannot be the leader of the pack!"

"Yes, he can!" her uncle replied. "There is no law that says that the leader has to be a coyote. To be the leader of the pack, you only have to defeat the current leader."

"He's right!" a council member said. "Ding is the only one who is strong enough to defeat Scout!"

"Then it's agreed!" her uncle said as the council all nodded. "I will go immediately to get him!"

Wendy and the sergeant were coming out of the house when they spotted Ding chasing after a coyote. They tried calling for him, but Ding continued to chase the coyote. The sergeant looked at Wendy. "Don't worry, I will go and get him!" The sergeant grabbed his gun belt and left to find Ding.

"Good! You brought her back!" Scout said, smiling at his soon-to-be bride.

"I will never marry you!" Snow yelled.

Scout came down off the rock he was sitting on. "Ohh! Yes, you will marry me, and you will give birth to my offspring. And together, we will hunt on the farmer's land and feast on their livestock!"

"If we kill the farmer's livestock, they will hunt us down and kill us!" Snow yelled. "You are no leader! You are a fool pretending to be one!"

Scout slapped Snow across her face. "You will show respect to your leader and soon-to-be husband!" As Scout stood there over Snow, he felt something hit him in the ribs and sent him rolling across the ground.

"Are you okay?" Ding asked Snow as he nudged her.

"How dare you attack me!" Scout growled as he picked himself up off the ground. "I am the leader of the pack, and no one will disrespect me like that! Especially a farm dog!"

"Respect? You don't deserve it!" Ding answered as he helped Snow off the ground. "Look around you! Your own family doesn't even respect you!" Ding said as he pointed to the other coyotes around them. "They are afraid of you! You will never get respect from them or yourself through fear!"

Scout stood there looking around at the other coyotes. He could see the fear in their faces; even his own brothers were afraid. As he looked at them, one by one, they turned their backs to him. "I am your leader! How dare you disrespect me like this!" he yelled in anger. "You! You are responsible for this disrespect!"

Scout lunged toward Ding, only to be thrown to the ground again. Scout quickly got back to his feet and charged at Ding. Ding grabbed Scout by his neck and flung him to the ground.

"I don't want to fight you!" Ding said. "But if you are going to be the leader of this family, you have to earn their respect!"

"I will have their respect once I kill you!" Scout yelled as he attacked Ding.

Ding grabbed Scout by his neck and flipped him over, causing Scout to land hard on his back.

"Enough brother!" Bones yelled as he stepped in between Ding and Scout. "You have been defeated!" Bones looked over to Snow and her uncle. "Scout is not the leader of the pack. He did not fight the chief in a fair fight but attacked him from behind, killing him instantly!" Bones looked back over to his brother Scout still trying to get back on his feet. "Brother, Ding is right! Even when we were just puppies, everyone was afraid of you, and the chief gave you a chance to finally be someone who could be respected, and you pay him back by ambushing him. You thought Tails and I were helping that day, but we were not. We were running away from you! The chief was even going to let you come home, come back to the family. I'm sorry you have to hear this, but Tails and I no longer consider you family because of the way you treat us and everyone here. We are done being afraid of you!"

As Bones turned away from Scout, he charged at Bones. Ding quickly intercepted Scout. Bones and Tails both ran to their brother Scout who was lying there, dying from the fatal blow delivered from Ding.

"I see now you were right," Scout said, gasping for air. "I was a horrible brother to you and everyone else!"

"I'm sorry!" Ding said to Tails and Bones. "I was just trying to protect you!"

Bones walked over to Ding and hugged him. "It's okay, brother."

"Ding!"

Everyone turned to see the sergeant walking toward Ding. All the coyotes were in shock and didn't know whether to run or stay. Seeing that the pack was looking for guidance on what to do, Snow began walking alongside the sergeant as he approached Ding.

"I saw what happened," the sergeant said as he knelt down in front of Ding. "You had to make a hard decision. And it looks like you are still making friends!" The sergeant looked over at the chief and Scout's bodies. "Well, we can't just leave them here. They need a proper burial." The sergeant stood up and walked over and picked up the two coyotes' bodies. "Come on, Ding, and you can bring your friends too."

As the sergeant walked away carrying the chief and Scout in his arms, Ding and Snow led the pack back to the farm.

As the sergeant drove two grave markers into the ground, Tails and Bones sat next to their brother's grave while Snow lay by her father to say their goodbyes. The entire pack lowered their heads in respect for their lost family members. Later that night under the full moon, Ding and Snow said their vows to each other in front of the family.

*****

"Now I understand!" Scout said. "How family and respect are the same!"

"Now!" Sassy said, slapping Scout on the back of his head. "After everyone kept telling you!"

"Shhh! Will you be quiet? We are trying to watch the wedding!" Jesse said, trying to get them to be quiet.

*****

"Bones, look!" Tails said, pointing into the night sky just above the newlyweds.

Just above Ding and Snow were the spirits of Scout, Sassy, Jesse, and the chief with Snow's mother. Scout looked down to his brothers and waved goodbye just before he turned around and raced Sassy back up the moonbeam.

Truth or Tall Tale

"Grandpa, you made that up!" Adain said, looking up at his grandfather from the floor.

Grandpa leaned forward in his rocking chair. "You grandkids asked me to tell you a story while we are waiting for Thanksgiving dinner, and I did. You have to decide whether or not the story is true."

Xavier was petting Grandpa's dog. "But his name is Brownie, not Ding?"

Atlas, the youngest of the grandsons, stood up. "I'm going to go ask Dad and see what he thinks about Grandpa's story!"

"Dinner is ready!" Grandma hollered from the back of the house.

As the grandsons left for the bathroom to wash up before dinner, Grandpa reached down, petting his old dog on the head. "Come on, you dingy dingo, let's go see if Snow's back with the puppies!"

ABOUT THE AUTHOR

Stewart is a proud father and stepfather of three boys and five girls. The experience of being a stepfather has allowed him to have his own extended family.

He has served in both the Army and Air Force and retired from the Army National Guard after twenty-two years of service. During this time, he traveled to several different countries and enjoyed experiencing new cultures and making new friends.

Ding and his extended family were written to show that your family is always with you and that you are never alone. Your family can be as big or small as you want it to be and made from the ones you call family.

No matter the likes or dislikes, color or race, and beliefs, your family is always there for you.